[redacted]

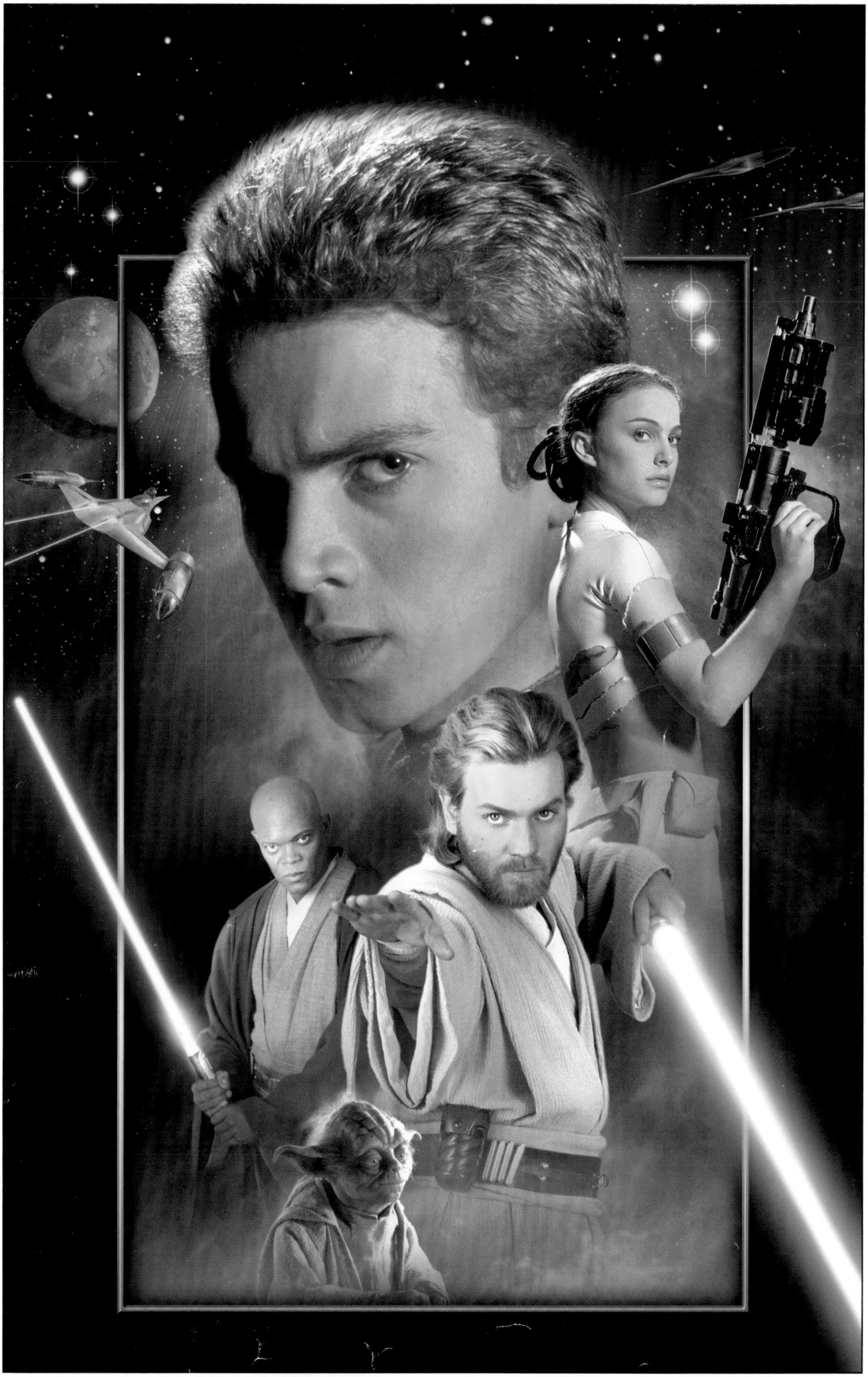

STAR WARS®
EPISODE II
ATTACK OF THE CLONES™

VOLUME THREE

ADAPTED BY
HENRY GILROY

BASED ON THE ORIGINAL STORY BY
GEORGE LUCAS

AND THE SCREENPLAY BY
GEORGE LUCAS AND
JONATHAN HALES

PENCILS
JAN DUURSEMA

INKS
RAY KRYSSING

COLORS
DAVE MCCAIG

COLOR SEPARATOR
HAROLD MACKINNON

LETTERS
STEVE DUTRO

COVER ART
TSUNEO SANDA

DARK HORSE COMICS

Spotlight

VISIT US AT
www.abdopublishing.com

Reinforced library bound edition published in 2009 by Spotlight, a division of the ABDO Group, 8000 West 78th Street, Edina, Minnesota 55439. Spotlight produces high-quality reinforced library bound editions for schools and libraries. Published by agreement with Dark Horse Comics, Inc., and Lucasfilm Ltd.

Library of Congress Cataloging-in-Publication Data

Gilroy, Henry.
  Episode II : attack of the clones / story, George Lucas ; script, Henry Gilroy ; pencils, Jan Duursema ; inks, Ray Kryssing ; colors, Dave McCaig ; letters, Steve Dutro. -- Reinforced library bound ed.
      p. cm. -- (Star Wars)
  ISBN 978-1-59961-612-4 (v. 1) -- ISBN 978-1-59961-613-1 (v. 2) – ISBN 978-1-59961-614-8 (v. 3) -- ISBN 978-1-59961-615-5 (v. 4)
  1. Graphic novels. [1. Graphic novels.] I. Lucas, George, 1944- II. Duursema, Jan, ill. III. Kryssing, Ray. IV. McCaig, Dave. V. Dutro, Steve. VI. Star wars, episode II, attack of the clones (Motion picture) VII. Title.
  PZ7.7.G55Epl 2009
  [Fic]--dc22
                            2008038311

Spotlight

All Spotlight books have reinforced library bindings and are manufactured in the United States of America.

Episode II

ATTACK OF THE CLONES

Volume 3

In his search for the person behind the assassination attempts on Senator Amidala, Jedi Obi-Wan Kenobi is led to the planet Kamino.

On Kamino, Obi-Wan discovers an army of clones is being built for the Republic—precisely the issue to which Amidala is opposed—based on the genetic structure of bounty hunter Jango Fett. Still on the planet, Fett executes a narrow escape when he discovers that Obi-Wan has found the clones.

Meanwhile, on the planet Naboo, Padawan Anakin Skywalker continues to protect Senator Amidala—until he senses that his mother is suffering. Both Amidala and Anakin leave the safety of Naboo to aid her. . .

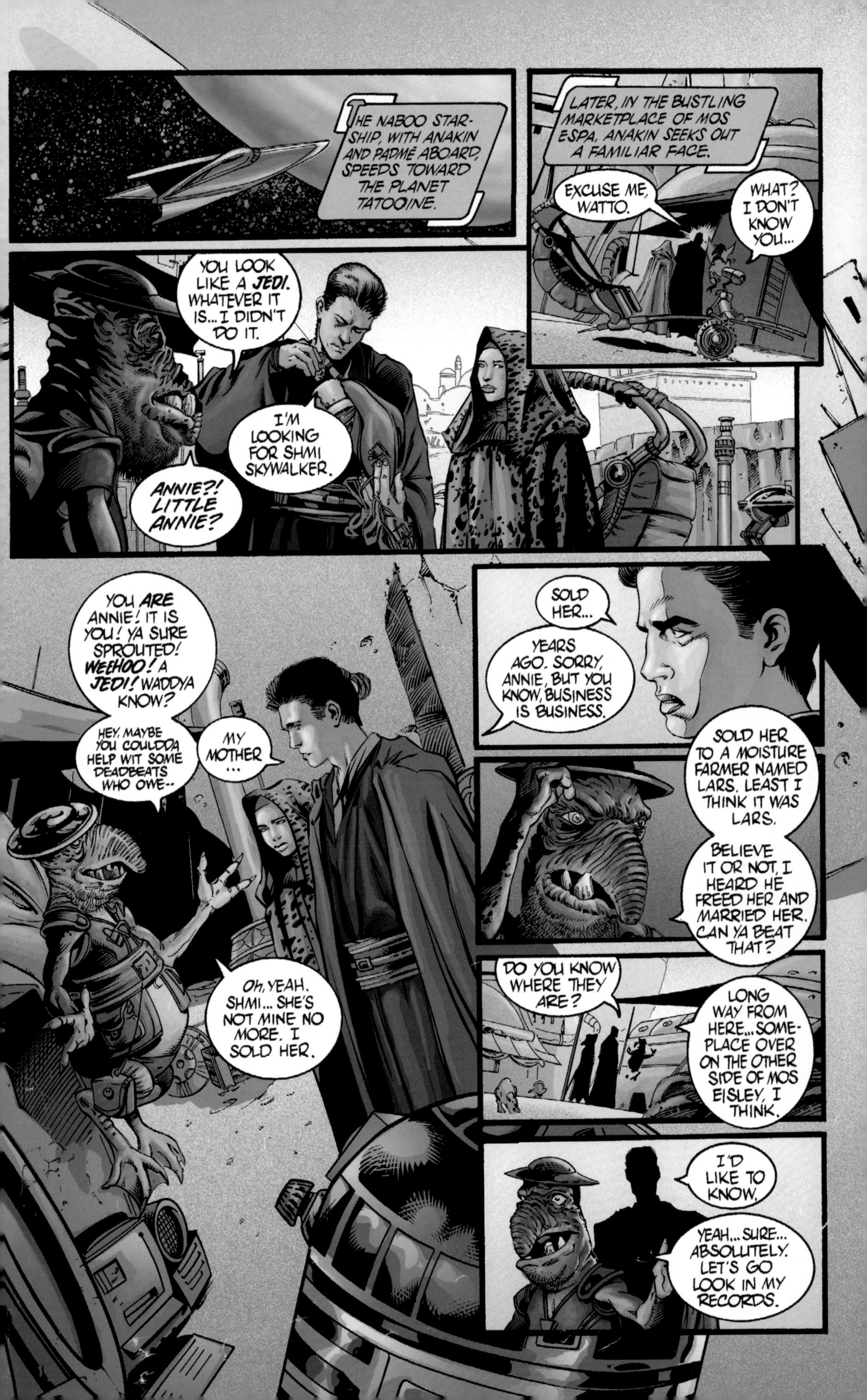
THE NABOO STAR-SHIP, WITH ANAKIN AND PADMÉ ABOARD, SPEEDS TOWARD THE PLANET TATOOINE.
LATER, IN THE BUSTLING MARKETPLACE OF MOS ESPA, ANAKIN SEEKS OUT A FAMILIAR FACE.
EXCUSE ME, WATTO.
WHAT? I DON'T KNOW YOU...
YOU LOOK LIKE A JEDI. WHATEVER IT IS... I DIDN'T DO IT.
I'M LOOKING FOR SHMI SKYWALKER.
ANNIE?! LITTLE ANNIE?
YOU ARE ANNIE! IT IS YOU! YA SURE SPROUTED! WEEHOO! A JEDI! WADDYA KNOW?
HEY, MAYBE YOU COULDDA HELP WIT SOME DEADBEATS WHO OWE--
MY MOTHER ...
Oh, YEAH. SHMI... SHE'S NOT MINE NO MORE. I SOLD HER.
SOLD HER...
YEARS AGO. SORRY, ANNIE, BUT YOU KNOW, BUSINESS IS BUSINESS.
SOLD HER TO A MOISTURE FARMER NAMED LARS. LEAST I THINK IT WAS LARS.
BELIEVE IT OR NOT, I HEARD HE FREED HER AND MARRIED HER. CAN YA BEAT THAT?
DO YOU KNOW WHERE THEY ARE?
LONG WAY FROM HERE... SOME-PLACE OVER ON THE OTHER SIDE OF MOS EISLEY, I THINK.
I'D LIKE TO KNOW.
YEAH... SURE... ABSOLUTELY. LET'S GO LOOK IN MY RECORDS.

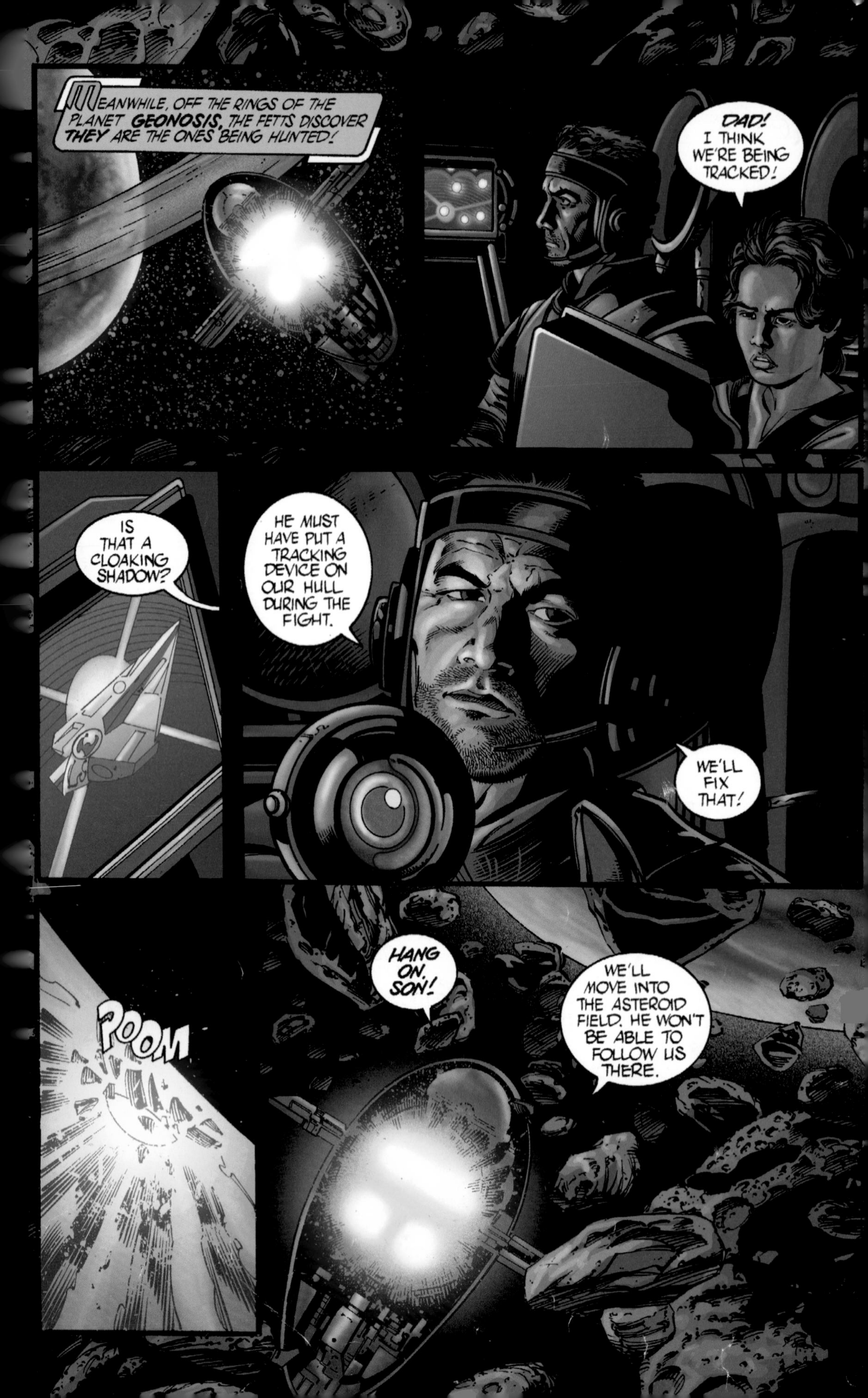
MEANWHILE, OFF THE RINGS OF THE PLANET GEONOSIS, THE FETTS DISCOVER THEY ARE THE ONES BEING HUNTED!
DAD! I THINK WE'RE BEING TRACKED!
IS THAT A CLOAKING SHADOW?
HE MUST HAVE PUT A TRACKING DEVICE ON OUR HULL DURING THE FIGHT.
WE'LL FIX THAT!
POOM
HANG ON, SON!
WE'LL MOVE INTO THE ASTEROID FIELD. HE WON'T BE ABLE TO FOLLOW US THERE.

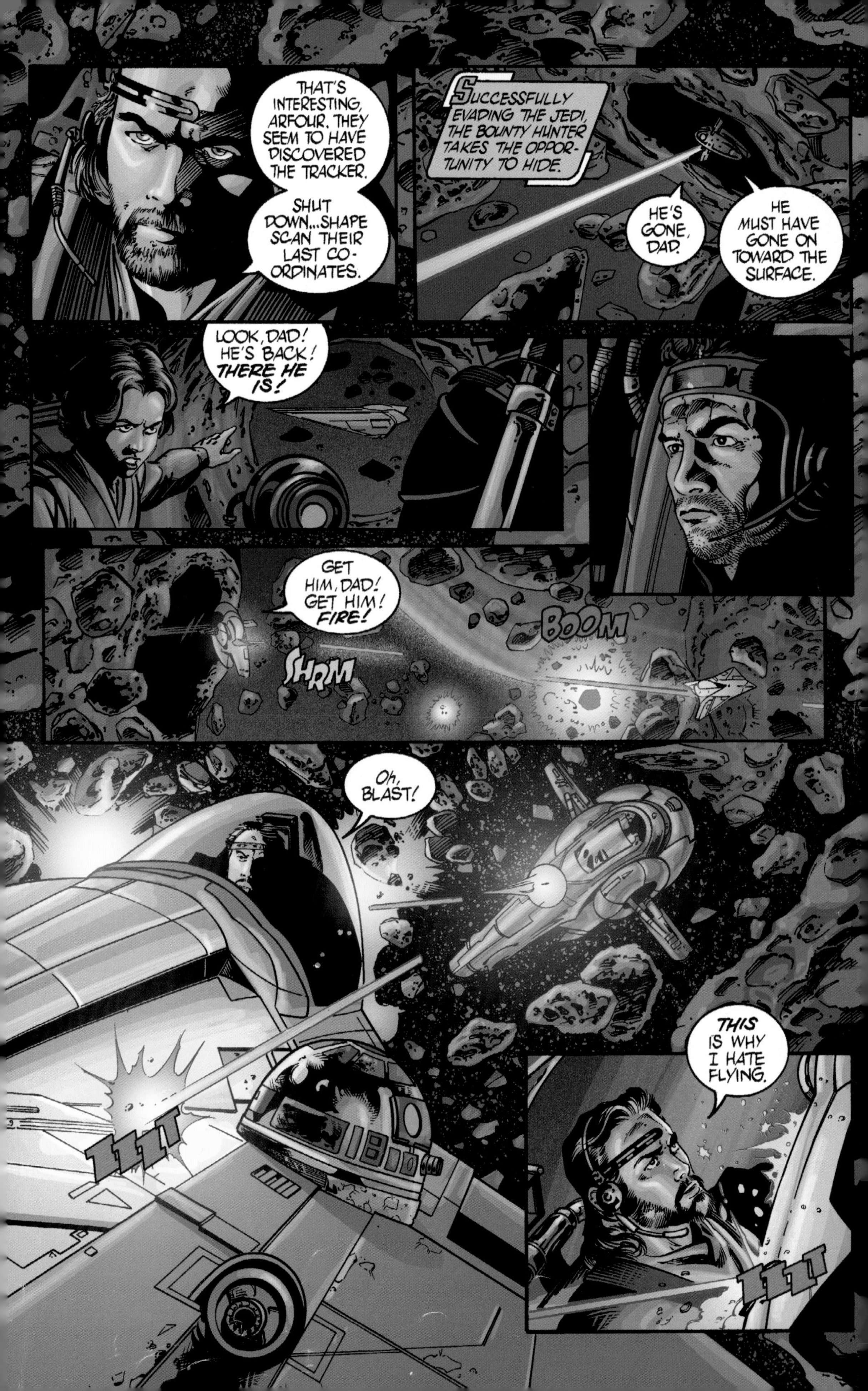
THAT'S INTERESTING, ARFOUR. THEY SEEM TO HAVE DISCOVERED THE TRACKER.
SHUT DOWN... SHAPE SCAN THEIR LAST CO-ORDINATES.
SUCCESSFULLY EVADING THE JEDI, THE BOUNTY HUNTER TAKES THE OPPORTUNITY TO HIDE.
HE'S GONE, DAD.
HE MUST HAVE GONE ON TOWARD THE SURFACE.
LOOK, DAD! HE'S BACK! THERE HE IS!
GET HIM, DAD! GET HIM! FIRE!
BOOM
SHRM
Oh, BLAST!
ZZZT
THIS IS WHY I HATE FLYING.
ZZZT

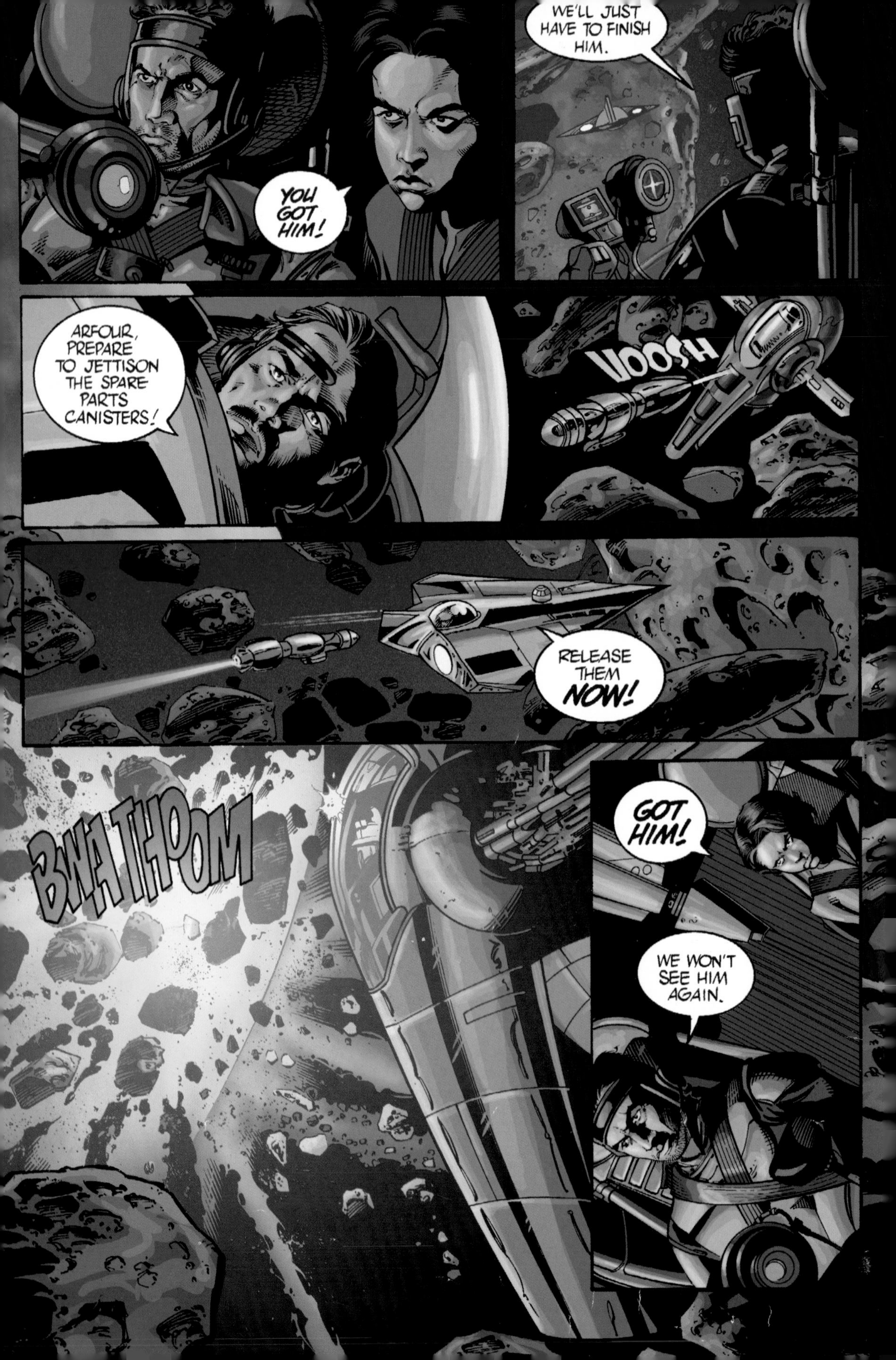
YOU GOT HIM!
WE'LL JUST HAVE TO FINISH HIM.
ARFOUR, PREPARE TO JETTISON THE SPARE PARTS CANISTERS!
VOOSH
RELEASE THEM NOW!
BWATHOOM
GOT HIM!
WE WON'T SEE HIM AGAIN.

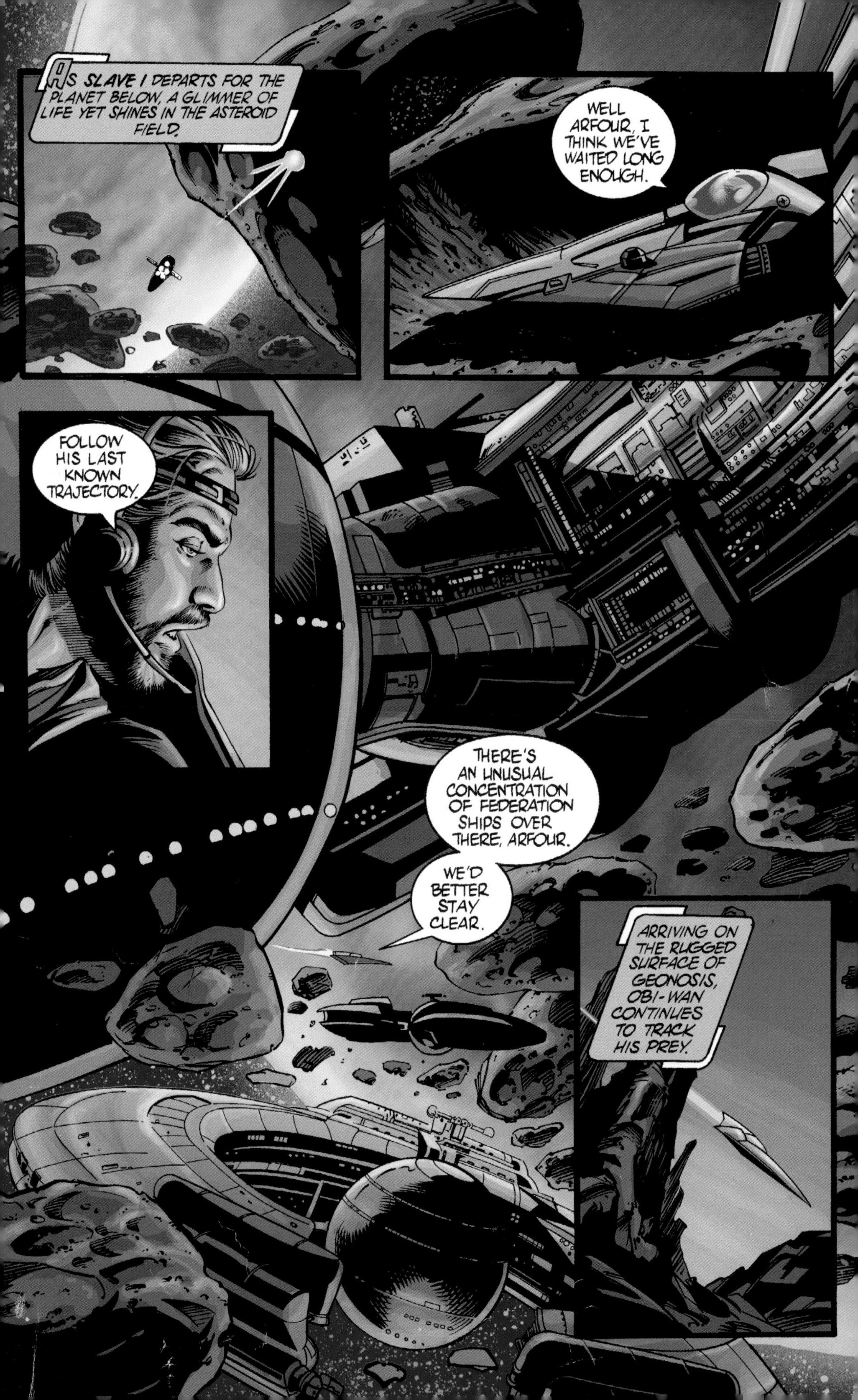
AS SLAVE I DEPARTS FOR THE PLANET BELOW, A GLIMMER OF LIFE YET SHINES IN THE ASTEROID FIELD.
WELL ARFOUR, I THINK WE'VE WAITED LONG ENOUGH.
FOLLOW HIS LAST KNOWN TRAJECTORY.
THERE'S AN UNUSUAL CONCENTRATION OF FEDERATION SHIPS OVER THERE, ARFOUR.
WE'D BETTER STAY CLEAR.
ARRIVING ON THE RUGGED SURFACE OF GEONOSIS, OBI-WAN CONTINUES TO TRACK HIS PREY.

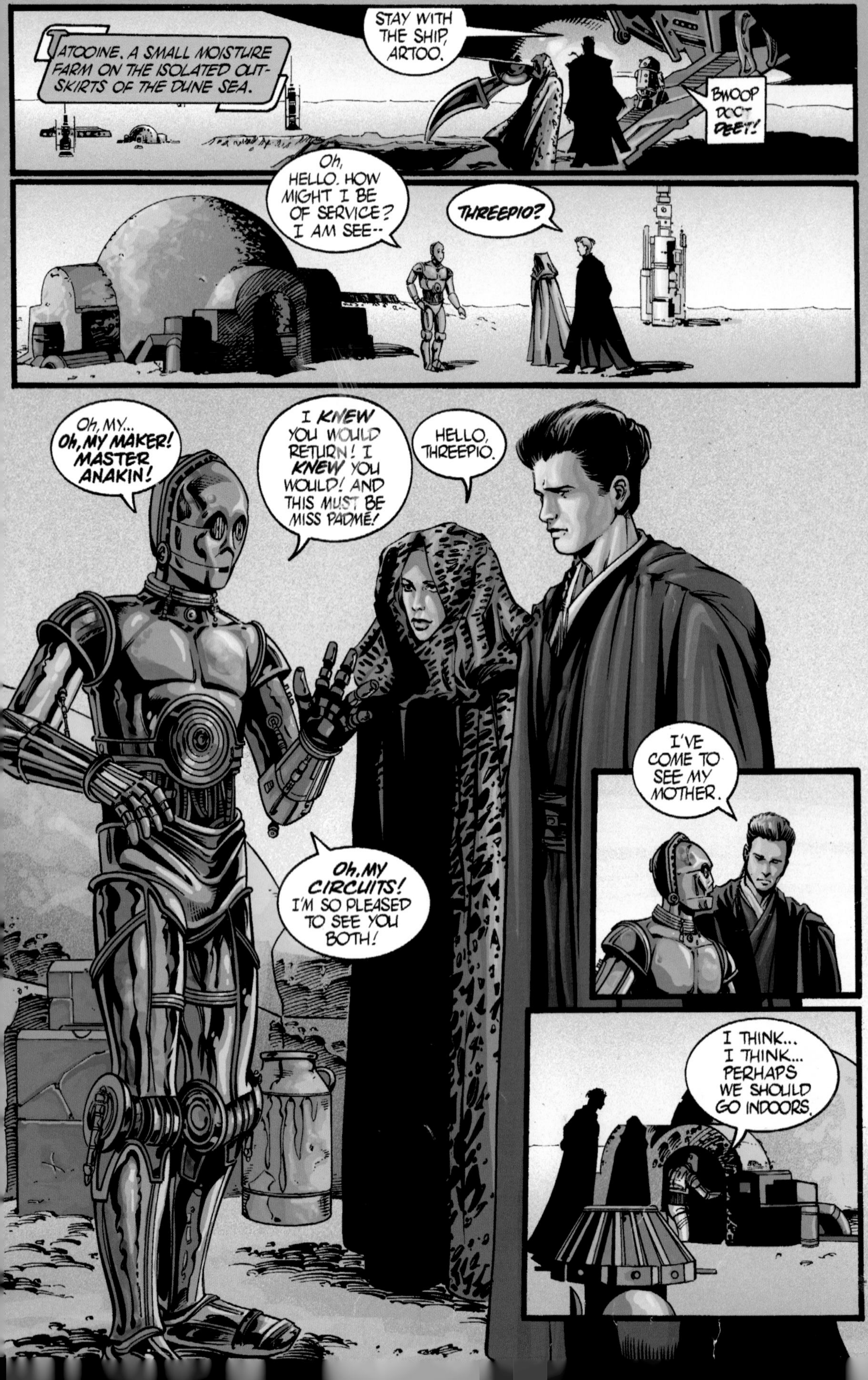

TATOOINE. A SMALL MOISTURE FARM ON THE ISOLATED OUT-SKIRTS OF THE DUNE SEA.
STAY WITH THE SHIP, ARTOO.
BWOOP DOOT DEET!
Oh, HELLO. HOW MIGHT I BE OF SERVICE? I AM SEE--
THREEPIO?
Oh, MY... Oh, MY MAKER! MASTER ANAKIN!
I KNEW YOU WOULD RETURN! I KNEW YOU WOULD! AND THIS MUST BE MISS PADMÉ!
HELLO, THREEPIO.
Oh, MY CIRCUITS! I'M SO PLEASED TO SEE YOU BOTH!
I'VE COME TO SEE MY MOTHER.
I THINK... I THINK... PERHAPS WE SHOULD GO INDOORS.

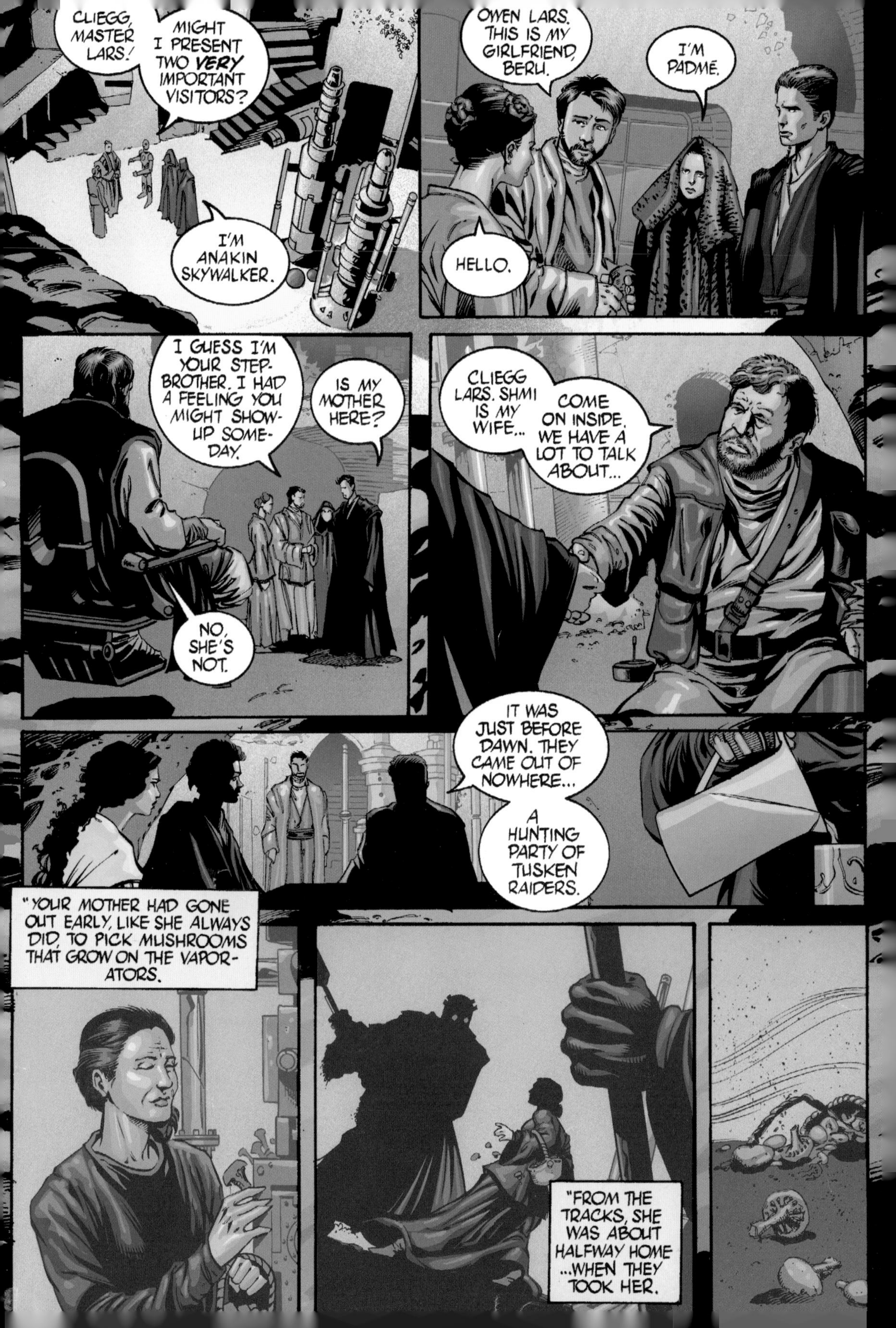
CLIEGG, MASTER LARS!
MIGHT I PRESENT TWO VERY IMPORTANT VISITORS?
I'M ANAKIN SKYWALKER.
OWEN LARS. THIS IS MY GIRLFRIEND, BERU.
I'M PADMÉ.
HELLO.
I GUESS I'M YOUR STEP-BROTHER. I HAD A FEELING YOU MIGHT SHOW-UP SOME-DAY.
IS MY MOTHER HERE?
NO, SHE'S NOT.
CLIEGG LARS. SHMI IS MY WIFE...
COME ON INSIDE. WE HAVE A LOT TO TALK ABOUT...
IT WAS JUST BEFORE DAWN. THEY CAME OUT OF NOWHERE...
A HUNTING PARTY OF TUSKEN RAIDERS.
"YOUR MOTHER HAD GONE OUT EARLY, LIKE SHE ALWAYS DID, TO PICK MUSHROOMS THAT GROW ON THE VAPOR-ATORS.
"FROM THE TRACKS, SHE WAS ABOUT HALFWAY HOME ...WHEN THEY TOOK HER.

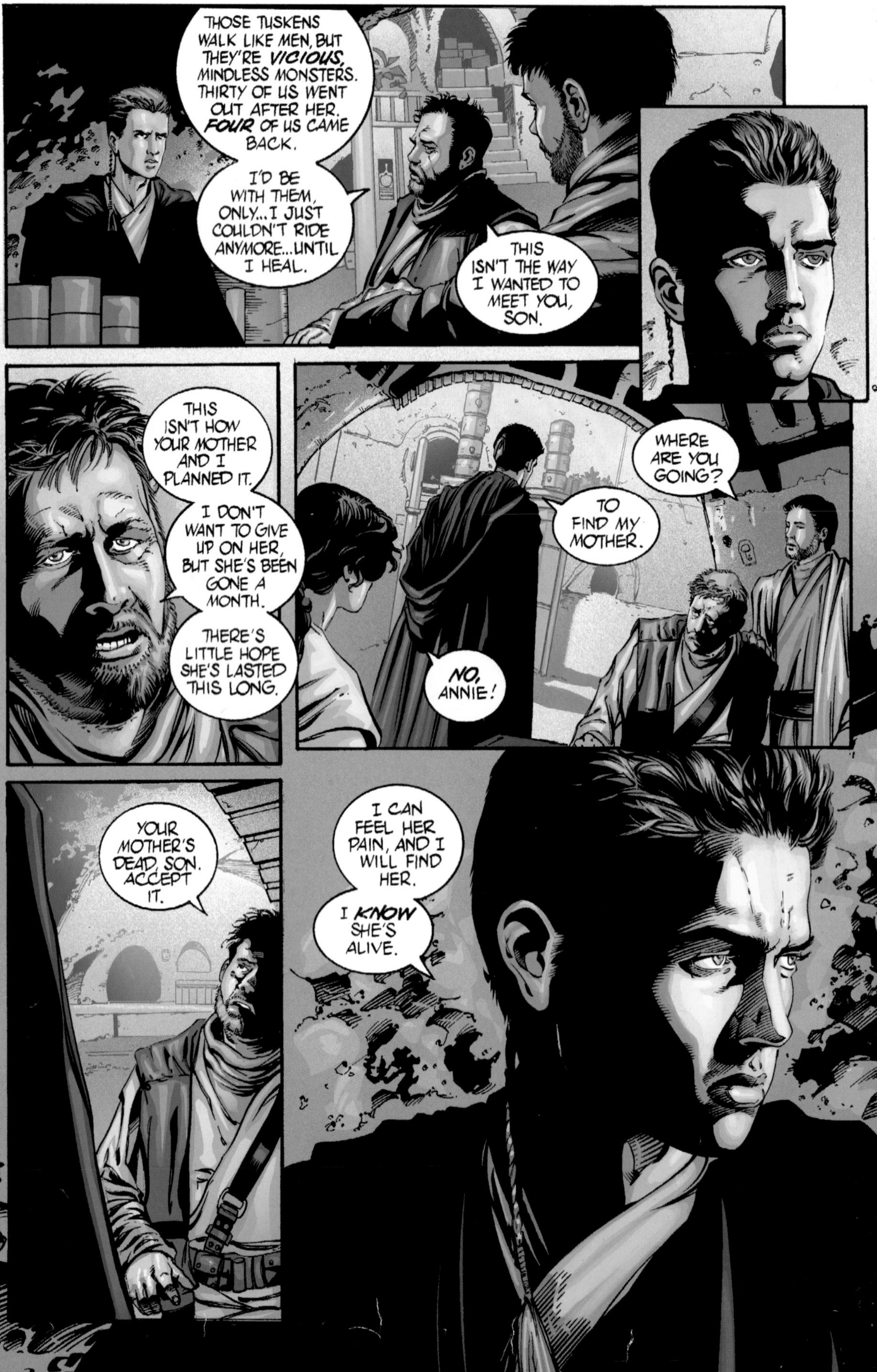
THOSE TUSKENS WALK LIKE MEN, BUT THEY'RE *VICIOUS*, MINDLESS MONSTERS. THIRTY OF US WENT OUT AFTER HER. *FOUR* OF US CAME BACK.
I'D BE WITH THEM, ONLY... I JUST COULDN'T RIDE ANYMORE... UNTIL I HEAL.
THIS ISN'T THE WAY I WANTED TO MEET YOU, SON.
THIS ISN'T HOW YOUR MOTHER AND I PLANNED IT.
I DON'T WANT TO GIVE UP ON HER, BUT SHE'S BEEN GONE A MONTH.
THERE'S LITTLE HOPE SHE'S LASTED THIS LONG.
WHERE ARE YOU GOING?
TO FIND MY MOTHER.
NO, ANNIE!
YOUR MOTHER'S DEAD, SON. ACCEPT IT.
I CAN FEEL HER PAIN, AND I WILL FIND HER.
I *KNOW* SHE'S ALIVE.

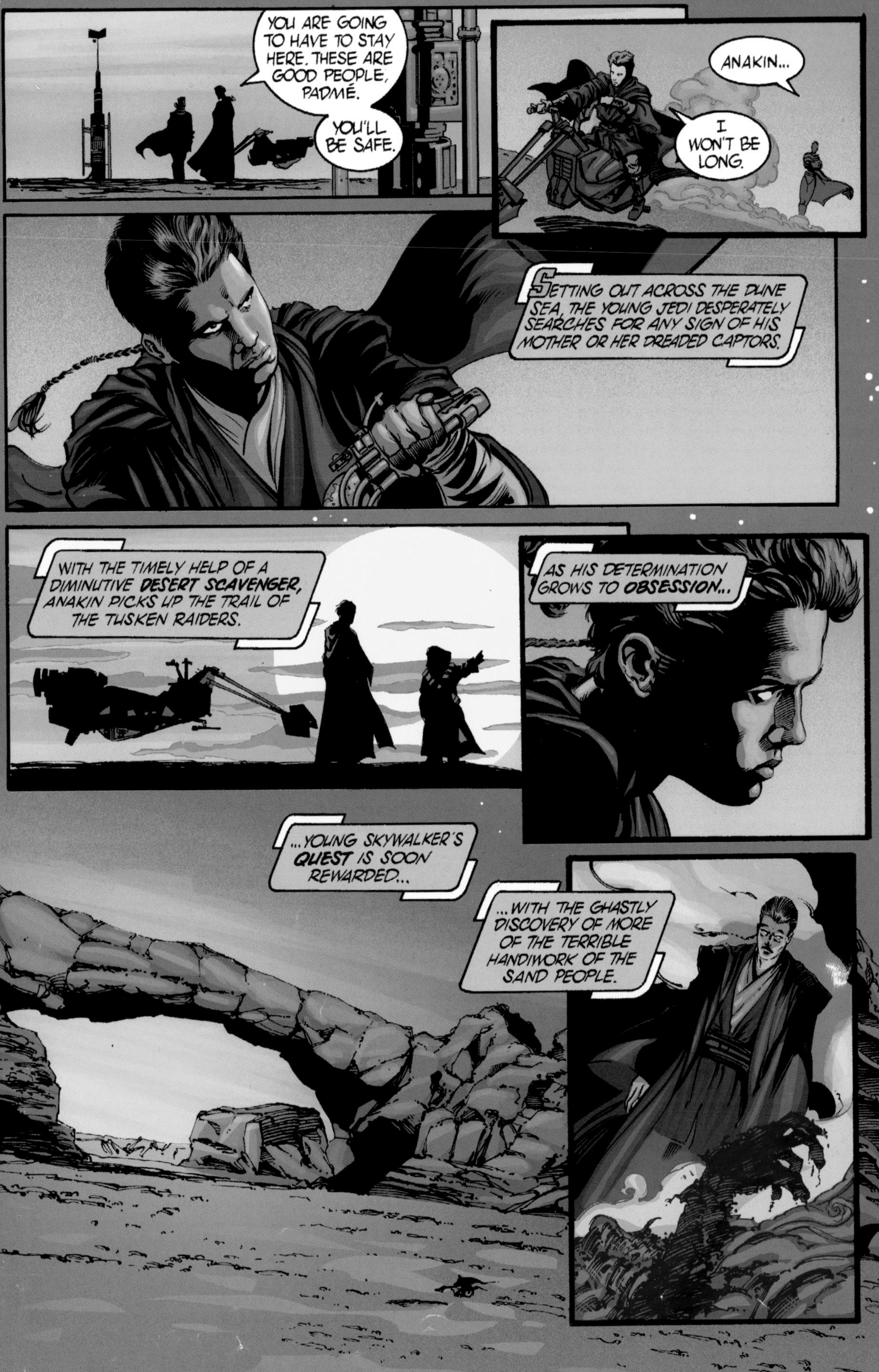
YOU ARE GOING TO HAVE TO STAY HERE. THESE ARE GOOD PEOPLE, PADMÉ.
YOU'LL BE SAFE.
ANAKIN...
I WON'T BE LONG.
SETTING OUT ACROSS THE DUNE SEA, THE YOUNG JEDI DESPERATELY SEARCHES FOR ANY SIGN OF HIS MOTHER OR HER DREADED CAPTORS.
WITH THE TIMELY HELP OF A DIMINUTIVE DESERT SCAVENGER, ANAKIN PICKS UP THE TRAIL OF THE TUSKEN RAIDERS.
AS HIS DETERMINATION GROWS TO OBSESSION...
...YOUNG SKYWALKER'S QUEST IS SOON REWARDED...
...WITH THE GHASTLY DISCOVERY OF MORE OF THE TERRIBLE HANDIWORK OF THE SAND PEOPLE.

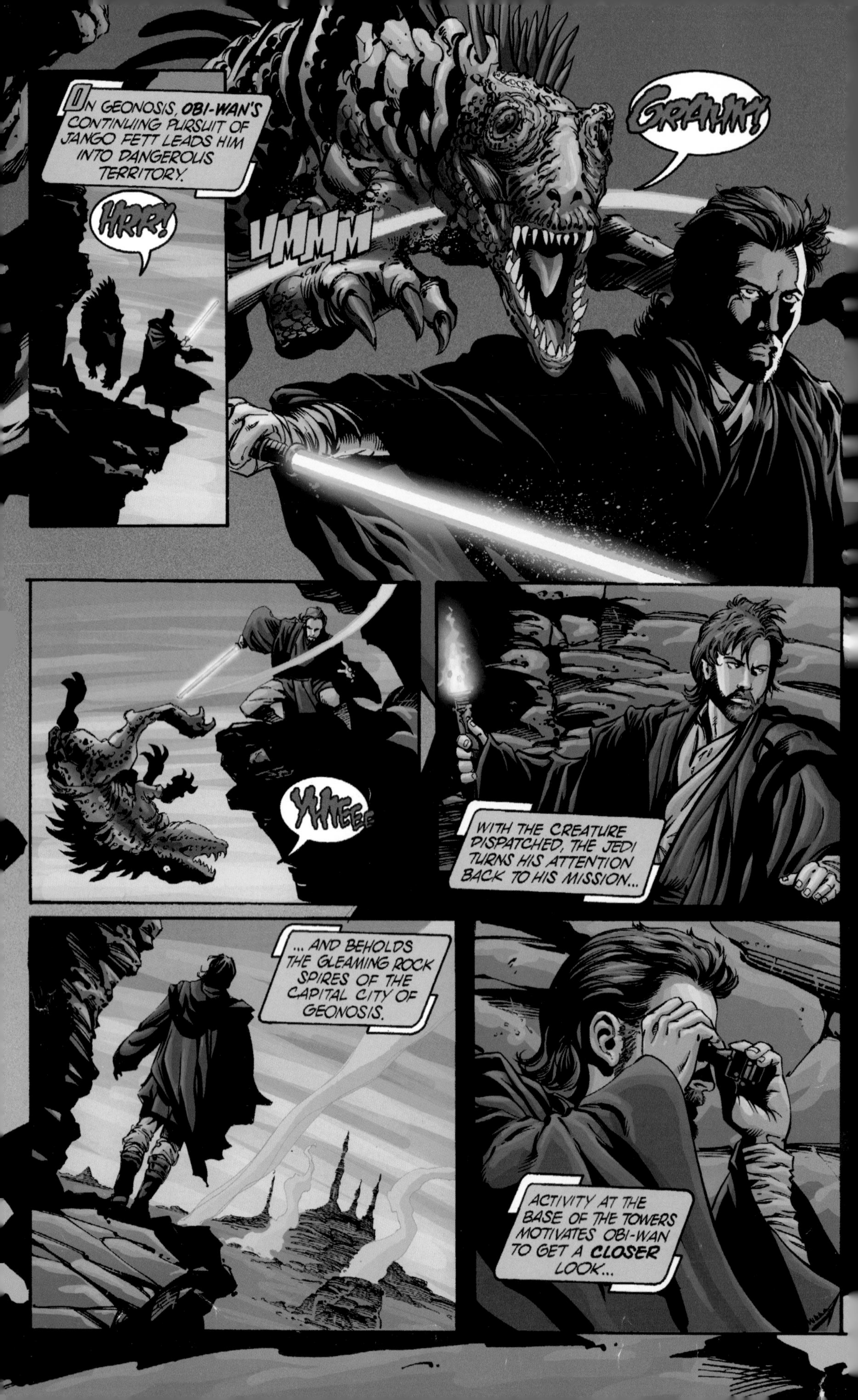
ON GEONOSIS, OBI-WAN'S CONTINUING PURSUIT OF JANGO FETT LEADS HIM INTO DANGEROUS TERRITORY.
HRRR!
GRAHH!
UMMM
YIIIEEE
WITH THE CREATURE DISPATCHED, THE JEDI TURNS HIS ATTENTION BACK TO HIS MISSION...
... AND BEHOLDS THE GLEAMING ROCK SPIRES OF THE CAPITAL CITY OF GEONOSIS.
ACTIVITY AT THE BASE OF THE TOWERS MOTIVATES OBI-WAN TO GET A CLOSER LOOK...

HUNDREDS OF FEDERATION BATTLESHIP CORES SIT PARKED IN FORMATION, AS IF *WAITING* FOR SOMETHING...

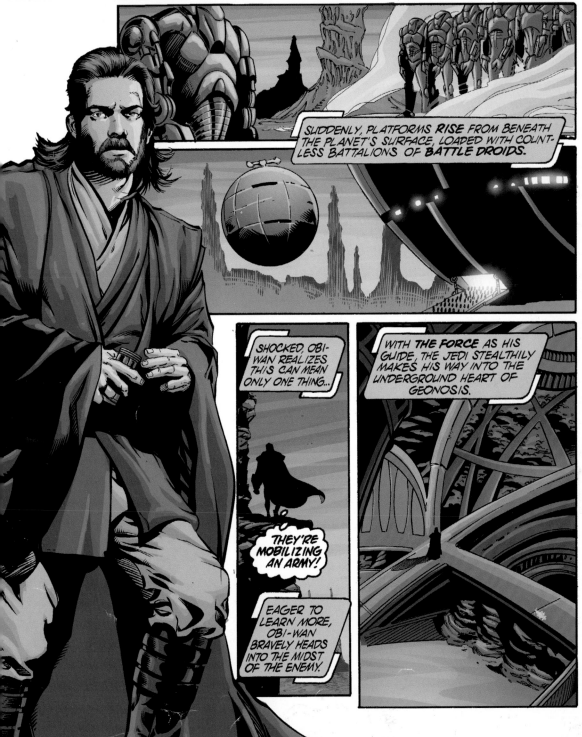

SUDDENLY, PLATFORMS *RISE* FROM BENEATH THE PLANET'S SURFACE, LOADED WITH COUNTLESS BATTALIONS OF *BATTLE DROIDS*.

SHOCKED, OBI-WAN REALIZES THIS CAN MEAN ONLY ONE THING...

THEY'RE MOBILIZING AN ARMY!

EAGER TO LEARN MORE, OBI-WAN BRAVELY HEADS INTO THE MIDST OF THE ENEMY.

WITH *THE FORCE* AS HIS GUIDE, THE JEDI STEALTHILY MAKES HIS WAY INTO THE UNDERGROUND HEART OF GEONOSIS.

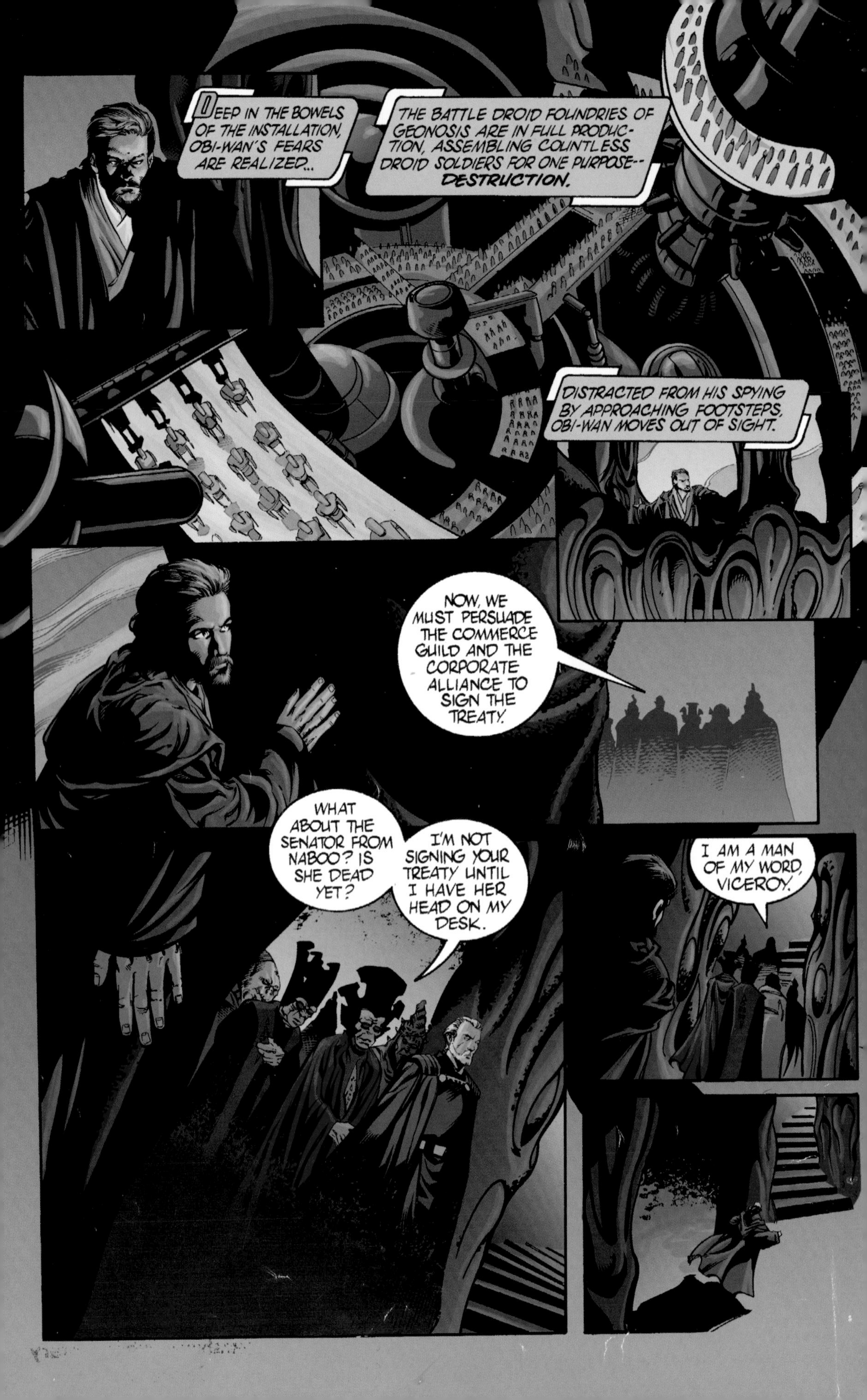
DEEP IN THE BOWELS OF THE INSTALLATION, OBI-WAN'S FEARS ARE REALIZED...
THE BATTLE DROID FOUNDRIES OF GEONOSIS ARE IN FULL PRODUCTION, ASSEMBLING COUNTLESS DROID SOLDIERS FOR ONE PURPOSE-- DESTRUCTION.
DISTRACTED FROM HIS SPYING BY APPROACHING FOOTSTEPS, OBI-WAN MOVES OUT OF SIGHT.
NOW, WE MUST PERSUADE THE COMMERCE GUILD AND THE CORPORATE ALLIANCE TO SIGN THE TREATY.
WHAT ABOUT THE SENATOR FROM NABOO? IS SHE DEAD YET?
I'M NOT SIGNING YOUR TREATY UNTIL I HAVE HER HEAD ON MY DESK.
I AM A MAN OF MY WORD, VICEROY.

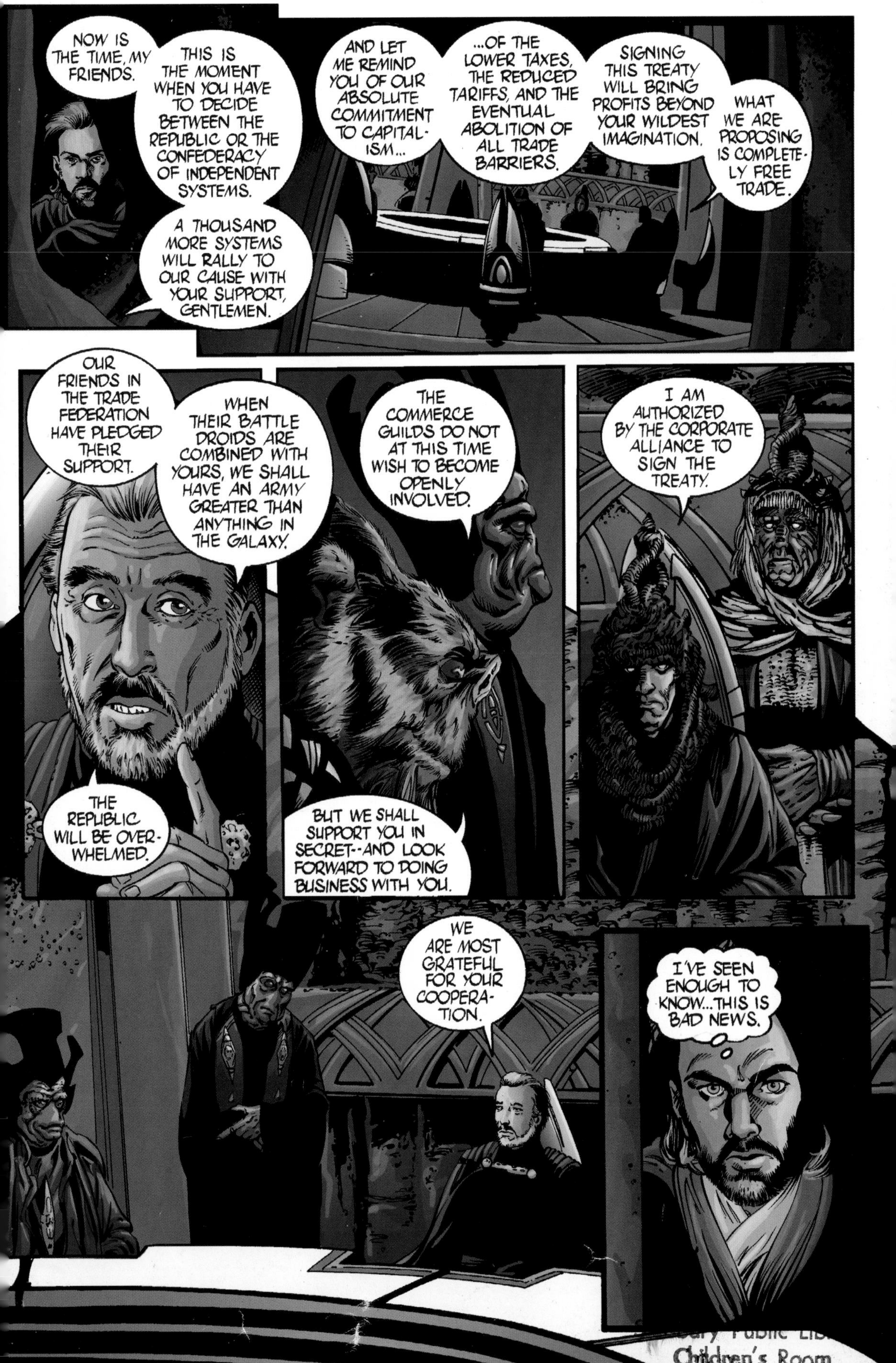
NOW IS THE TIME, MY FRIENDS.
THIS IS THE MOMENT WHEN YOU HAVE TO DECIDE BETWEEN THE REPUBLIC OR THE CONFEDERACY OF INDEPENDENT SYSTEMS.
A THOUSAND MORE SYSTEMS WILL RALLY TO OUR CAUSE WITH YOUR SUPPORT, GENTLEMEN.
AND LET ME REMIND YOU OF OUR ABSOLUTE COMMITMENT TO CAPITAL-ISM...
...OF THE LOWER TAXES, THE REDUCED TARIFFS, AND THE EVENTUAL ABOLITION OF ALL TRADE BARRIERS.
SIGNING THIS TREATY WILL BRING PROFITS BEYOND YOUR WILDEST IMAGINATION.
WHAT WE ARE PROPOSING IS COMPLETE-LY FREE TRADE.
OUR FRIENDS IN THE TRADE FEDERATION HAVE PLEDGED THEIR SUPPORT.
WHEN THEIR BATTLE DROIDS ARE COMBINED WITH YOURS, WE SHALL HAVE AN ARMY GREATER THAN ANYTHING IN THE GALAXY.
THE REPUBLIC WILL BE OVER-WHELMED.
THE COMMERCE GUILDS DO NOT AT THIS TIME WISH TO BECOME OPENLY INVOLVED.
BUT WE SHALL SUPPORT YOU IN SECRET--AND LOOK FORWARD TO DOING BUSINESS WITH YOU.
I AM AUTHORIZED BY THE CORPORATE ALLIANCE TO SIGN THE TREATY.
WE ARE MOST GRATEFUL FOR YOUR COOPERA-TION.
I'VE SEEN ENOUGH TO KNOW...THIS IS BAD NEWS.

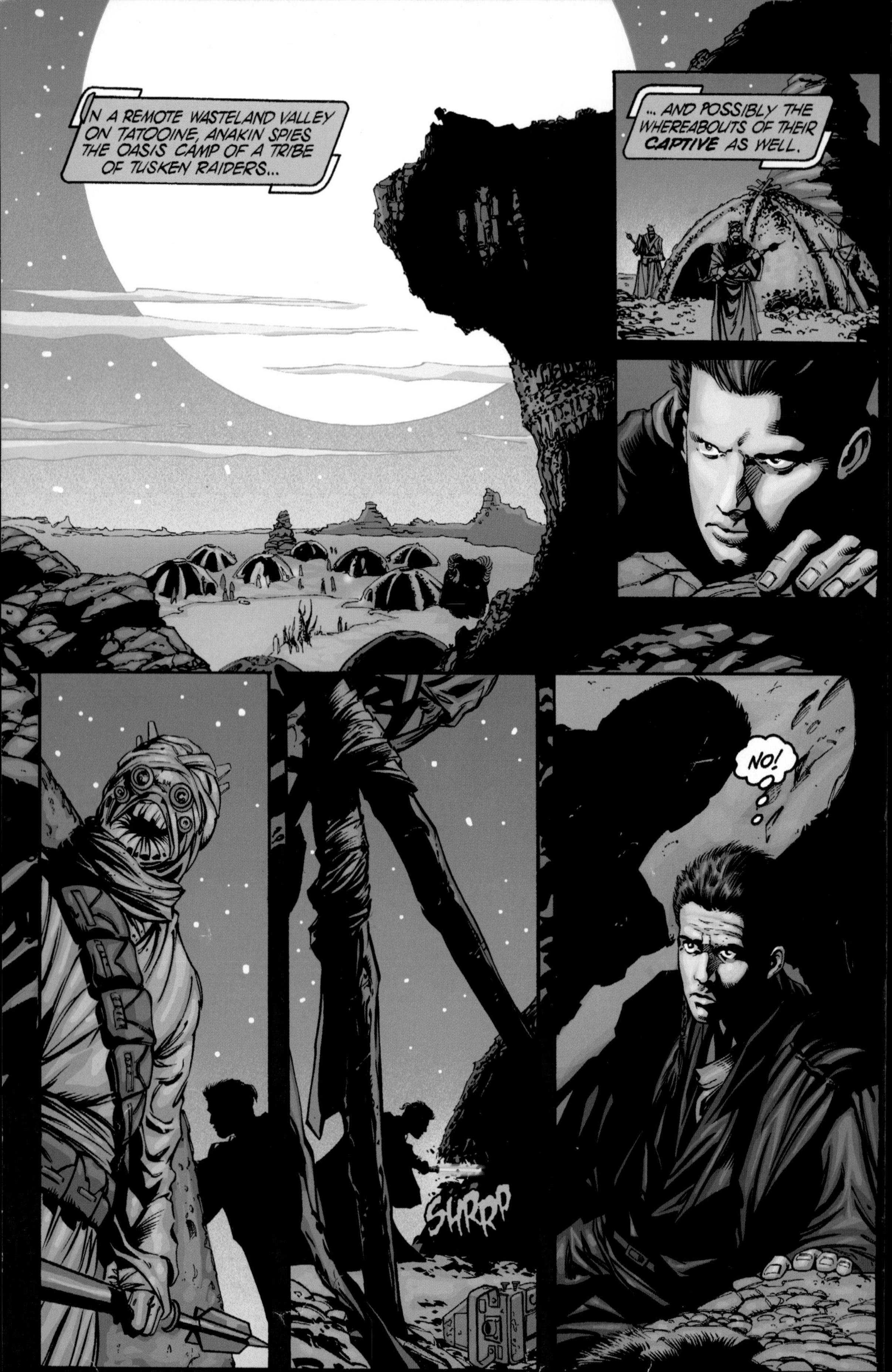
IN A REMOTE WASTELAND VALLEY ON TATOOINE, ANAKIN SPIES THE OASIS CAMP OF A TRIBE OF TUSKEN RAIDERS...
... AND POSSIBLY THE WHEREABOUTS OF THEIR CAPTIVE AS WELL.
SHRRP
NO!

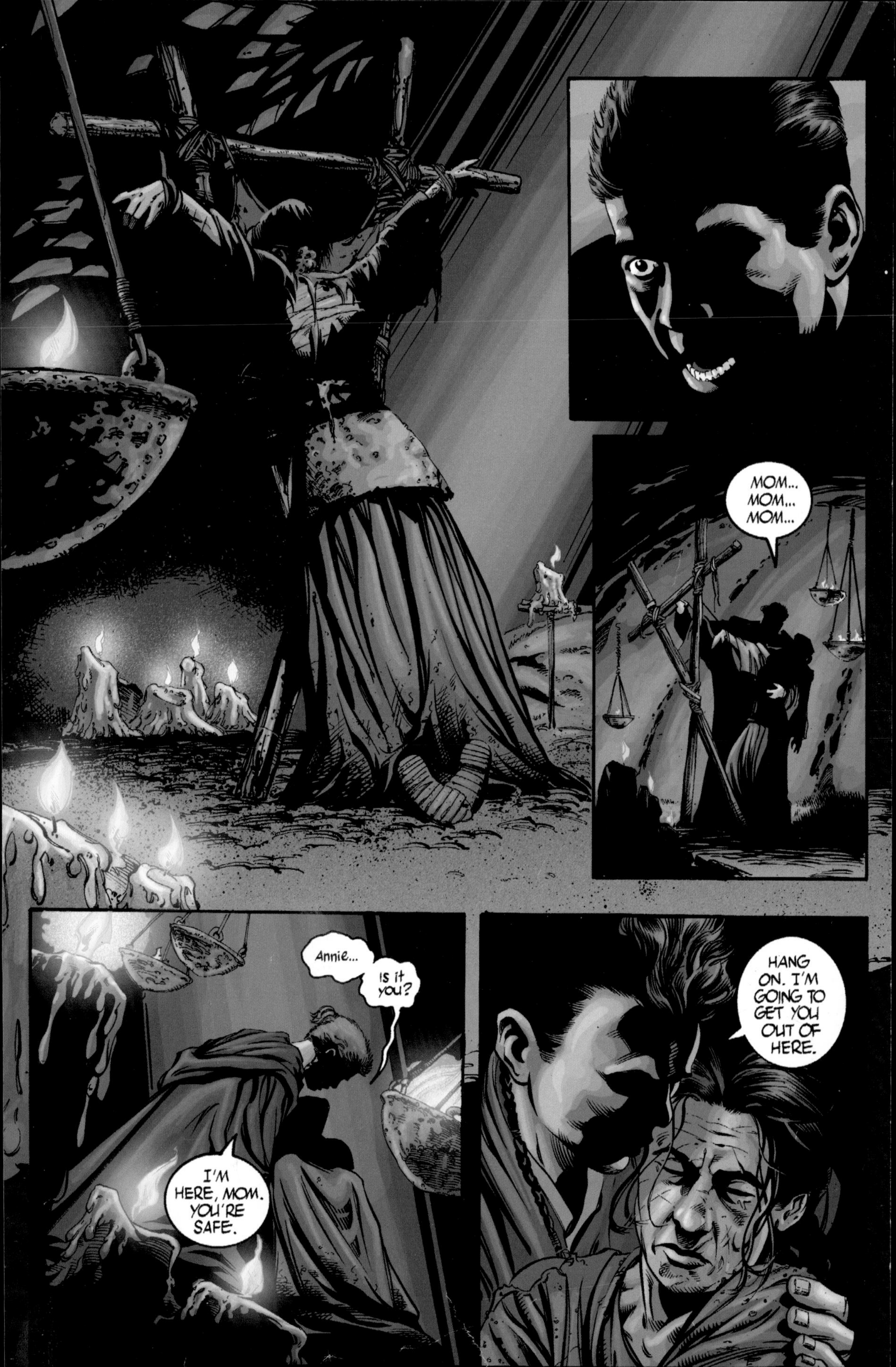
MOM... MOM... MOM...
Annie...
Is it you?
I'M HERE, MOM. YOU'RE SAFE.
HANG ON. I'M GOING TO GET YOU OUT OF HERE.

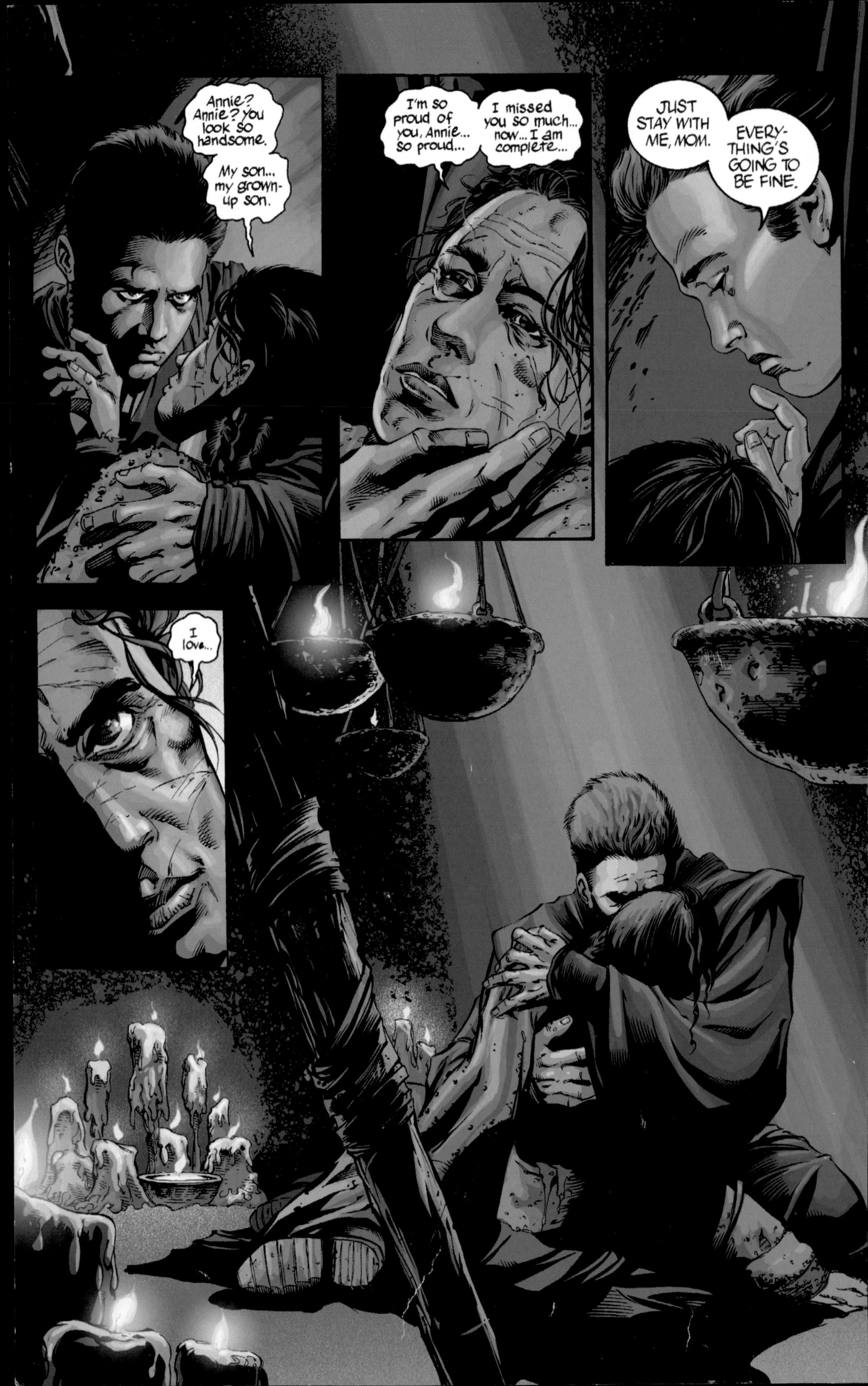
Annie? Annie? you look so handsome.
My son... my grown-up son.
I'm so proud of you, Annie... so proud...
I missed you so much... now... I am complete...
JUST STAY WITH ME, MOM.
EVERYTHING'S GOING TO BE FINE.
I love...

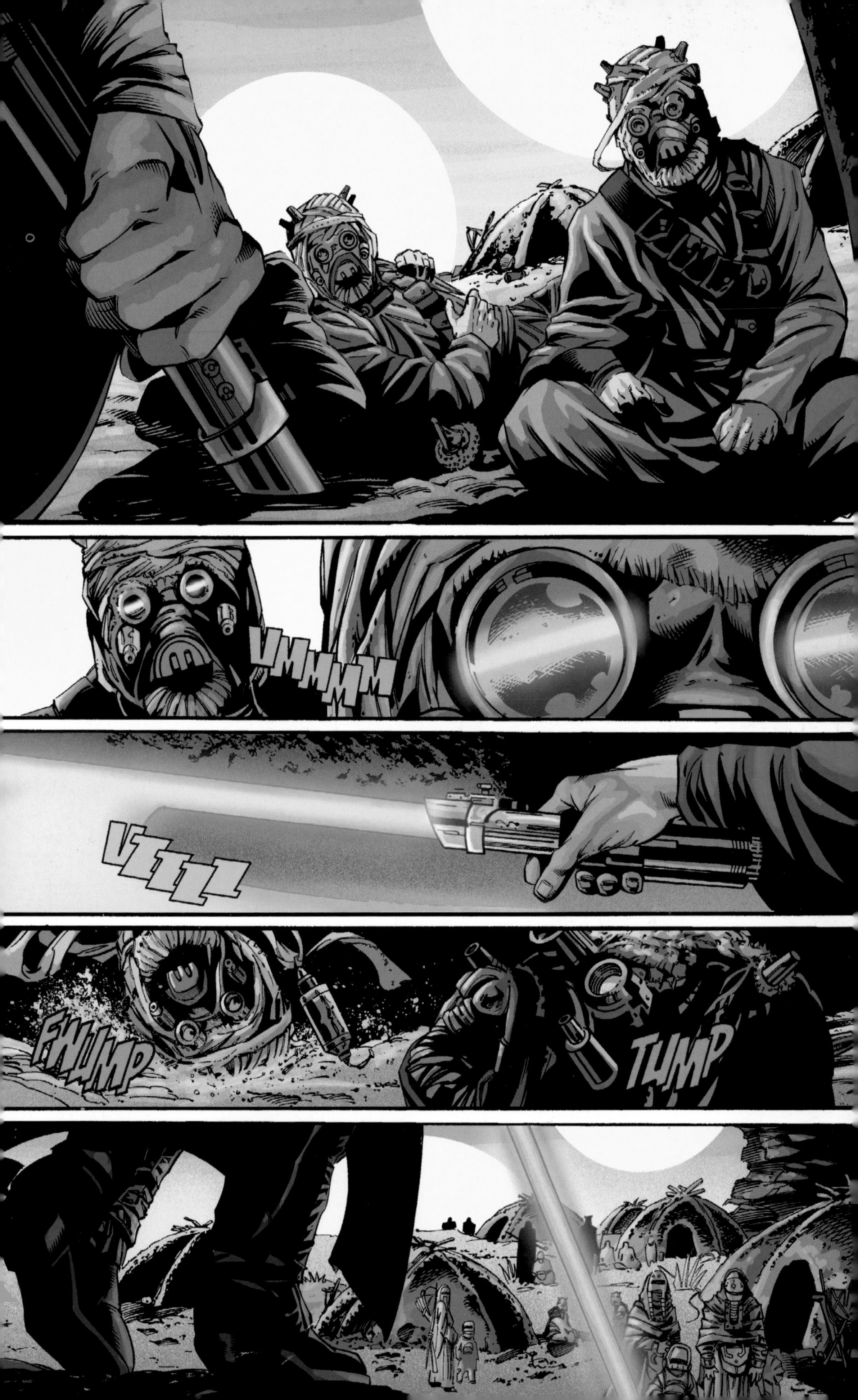
UMMMMM
VZZZZ
FWUMP
TUMP

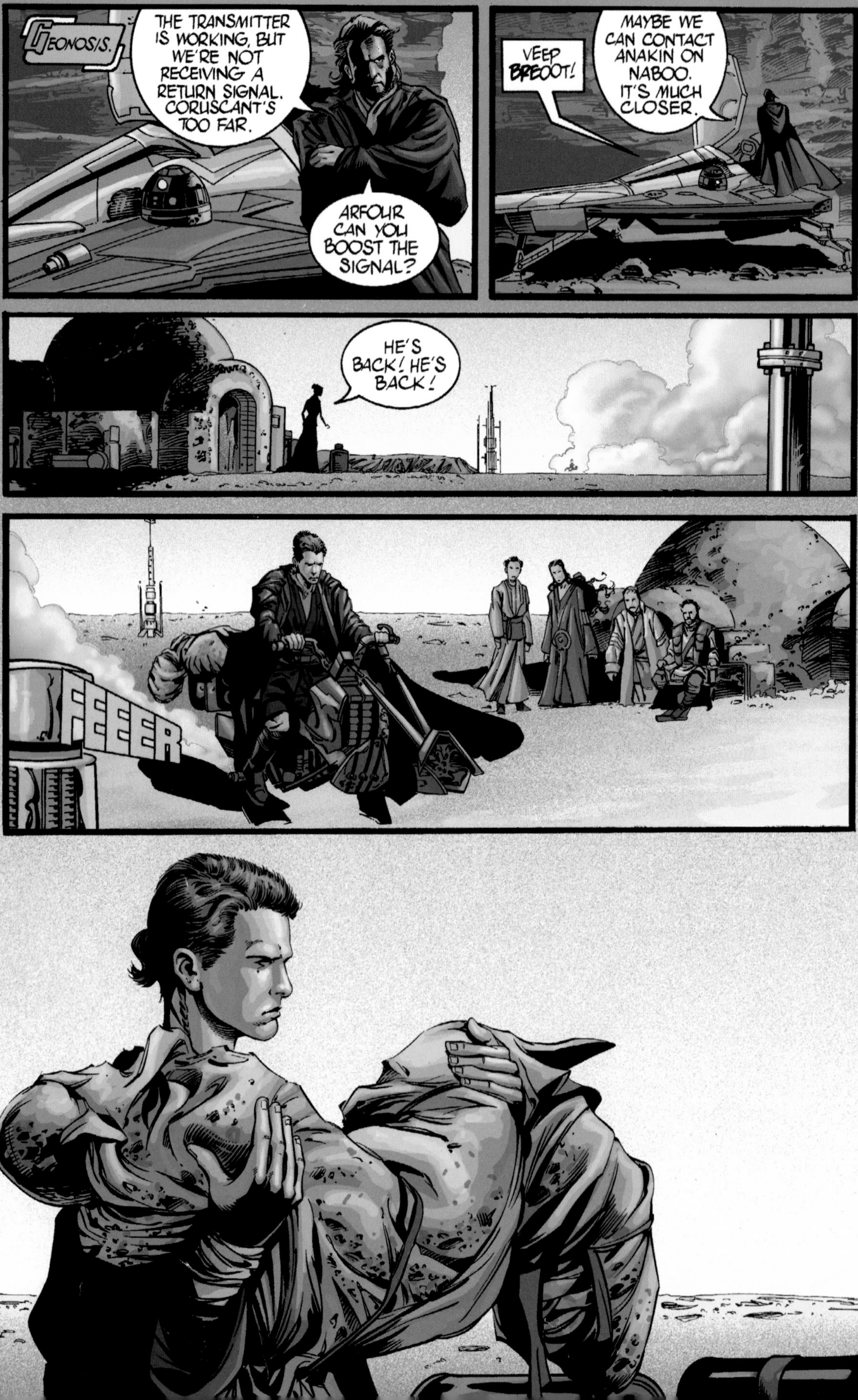
GEONOSIS.
THE TRANSMITTER IS WORKING, BUT WE'RE NOT RECEIVING A RETURN SIGNAL. CORUSCANT'S TOO FAR.
ARFOUR CAN YOU BOOST THE SIGNAL?
VEEP BREOOT!
MAYBE WE CAN CONTACT ANAKIN ON NABOO. IT'S MUCH CLOSER.
HE'S BACK! HE'S BACK!
FEEER

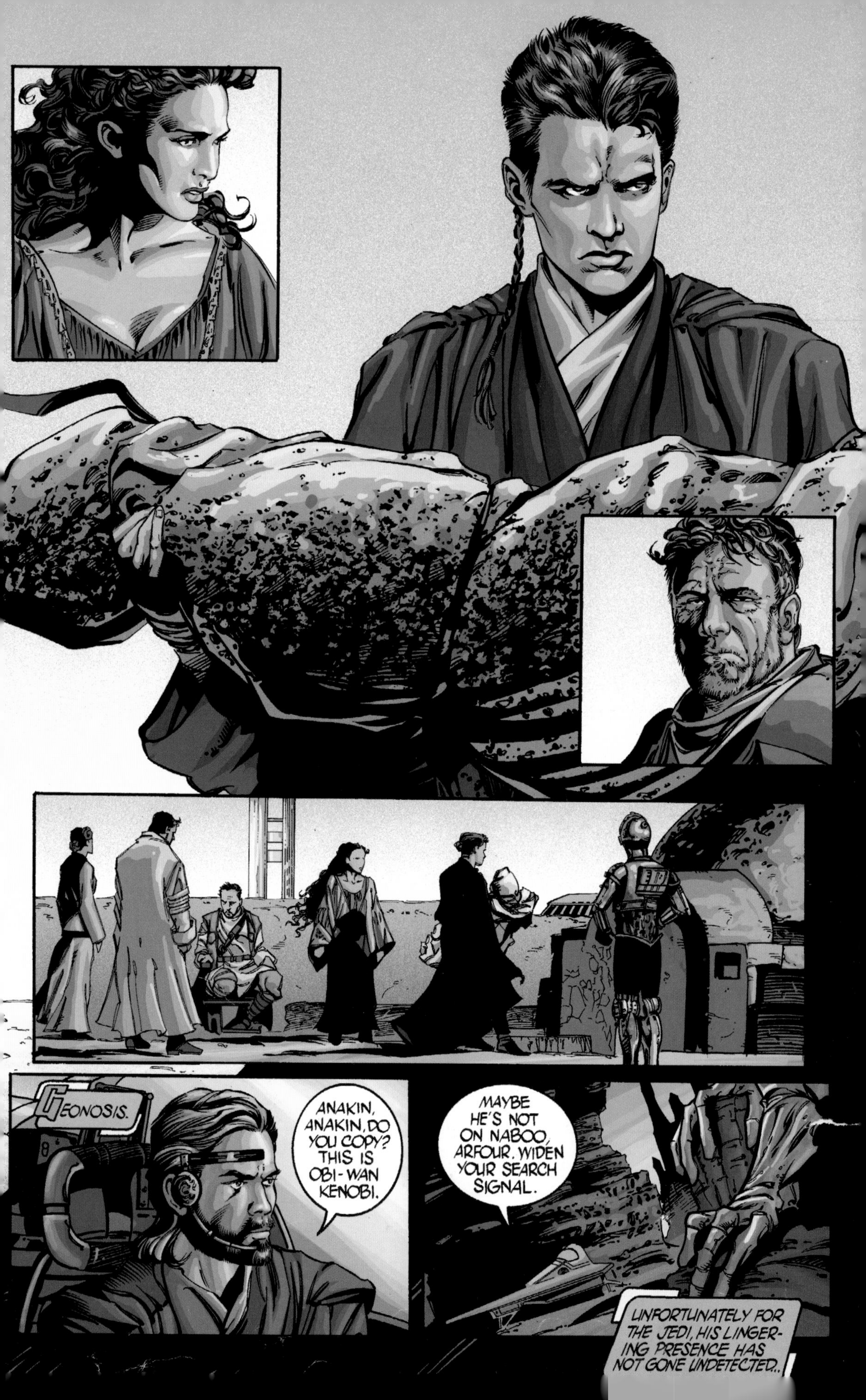
GEONOSIS.
ANAKIN, ANAKIN, DO YOU COPY? THIS IS OBI-WAN KENOBI.
MAYBE HE'S NOT ON NABOO, ARFOUR. WIDEN YOUR SEARCH SIGNAL.
UNFORTUNATELY FOR THE JEDI, HIS LINGERING PRESENCE HAS NOT GONE UNDETECTED...

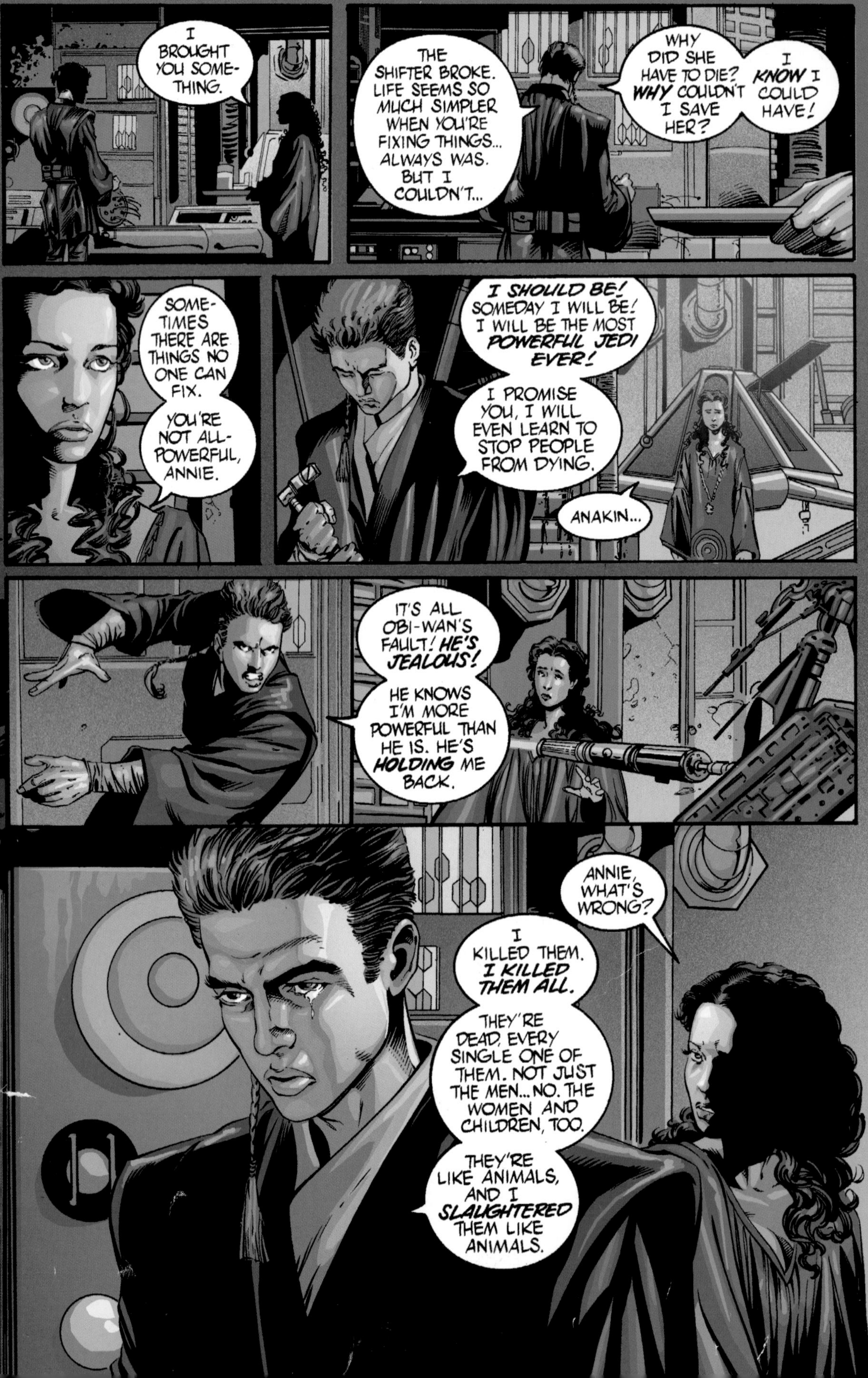
I BROUGHT YOU SOMETHING.
THE SHIFTER BROKE. LIFE SEEMS SO MUCH SIMPLER WHEN YOU'RE FIXING THINGS... ALWAYS WAS. BUT I COULDN'T...
WHY DID SHE HAVE TO DIE? *WHY* COULDN'T I SAVE HER?
I *KNOW* I COULD HAVE!
SOMETIMES THERE ARE THINGS NO ONE CAN FIX.
YOU'RE NOT ALL-POWERFUL, ANNIE.
I SHOULD BE! SOMEDAY I WILL BE! I WILL BE THE MOST *POWERFUL JEDI EVER!*
I PROMISE YOU, I WILL EVEN LEARN TO STOP PEOPLE FROM DYING.
ANAKIN...
IT'S ALL OBI-WAN'S FAULT! *HE'S JEALOUS!*
HE KNOWS I'M MORE POWERFUL THAN HE IS. HE'S *HOLDING* ME BACK.
ANNIE, WHAT'S WRONG?
I KILLED THEM. *I KILLED THEM ALL.*
THEY'RE DEAD, EVERY SINGLE ONE OF THEM. NOT JUST THE MEN... NO. THE WOMEN AND CHILDREN, TOO.
THEY'RE LIKE ANIMALS, AND I *SLAUGHTERED* THEM LIKE ANIMALS.

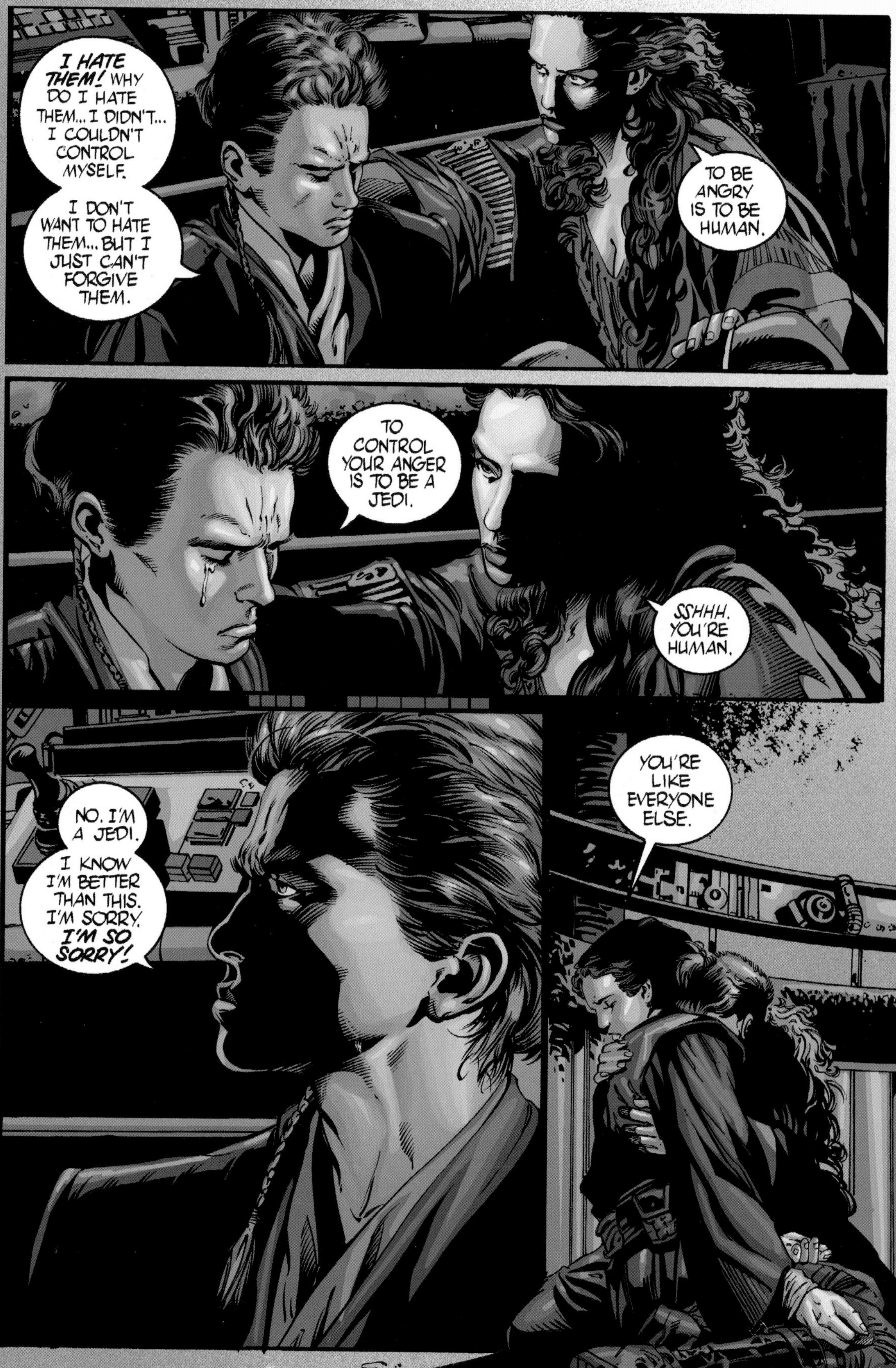
I HATE THEM! WHY DO I HATE THEM... I DIDN'T... I COULDN'T CONTROL MYSELF.
I DON'T WANT TO HATE THEM... BUT I JUST CAN'T FORGIVE THEM.
TO BE ANGRY IS TO BE HUMAN.
TO CONTROL YOUR ANGER IS TO BE A JEDI.
SSHHH. YOU'RE HUMAN.
NO. I'M A JEDI.
I KNOW I'M BETTER THAN THIS. I'M SORRY. I'M SO SORRY!
YOU'RE LIKE EVERYONE ELSE.

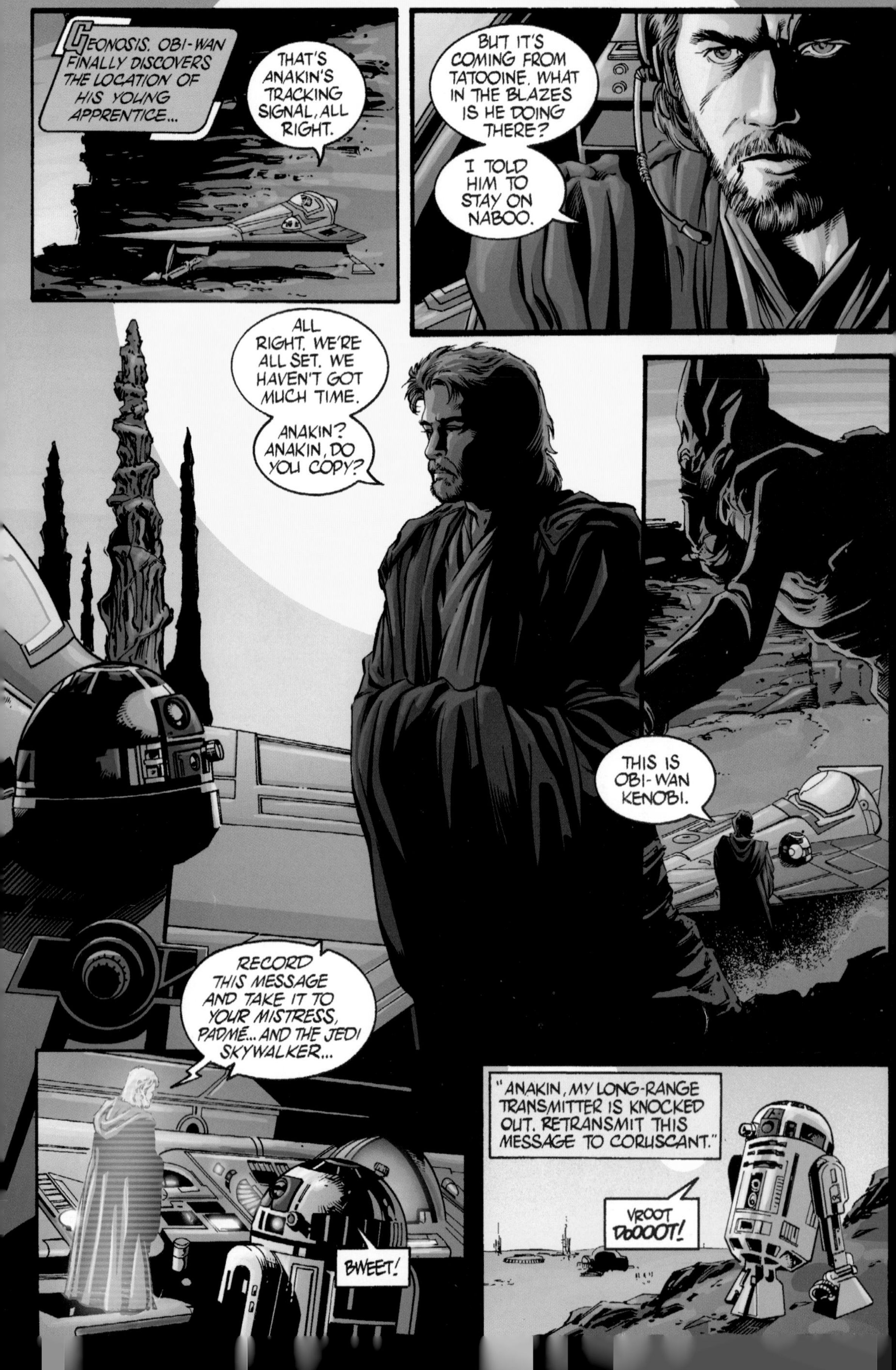
GEONOSIS. OBI-WAN FINALLY DISCOVERS THE LOCATION OF HIS YOUNG APPRENTICE...
THAT'S ANAKIN'S TRACKING SIGNAL, ALL RIGHT.
BUT IT'S COMING FROM TATOOINE. WHAT IN THE BLAZES IS HE DOING THERE?
I TOLD HIM TO STAY ON NABOO.
ALL RIGHT. WE'RE ALL SET. WE HAVEN'T GOT MUCH TIME.
ANAKIN? ANAKIN, DO YOU COPY?
THIS IS OBI-WAN KENOBI.
RECORD THIS MESSAGE AND TAKE IT TO YOUR MISTRESS, PADMÉ... AND THE JEDI SKYWALKER...
BWEET!
"ANAKIN, MY LONG-RANGE TRANSMITTER IS KNOCKED OUT. RETRANSMIT THIS MESSAGE TO CORUSCANT."
VROOT DOOOOT!

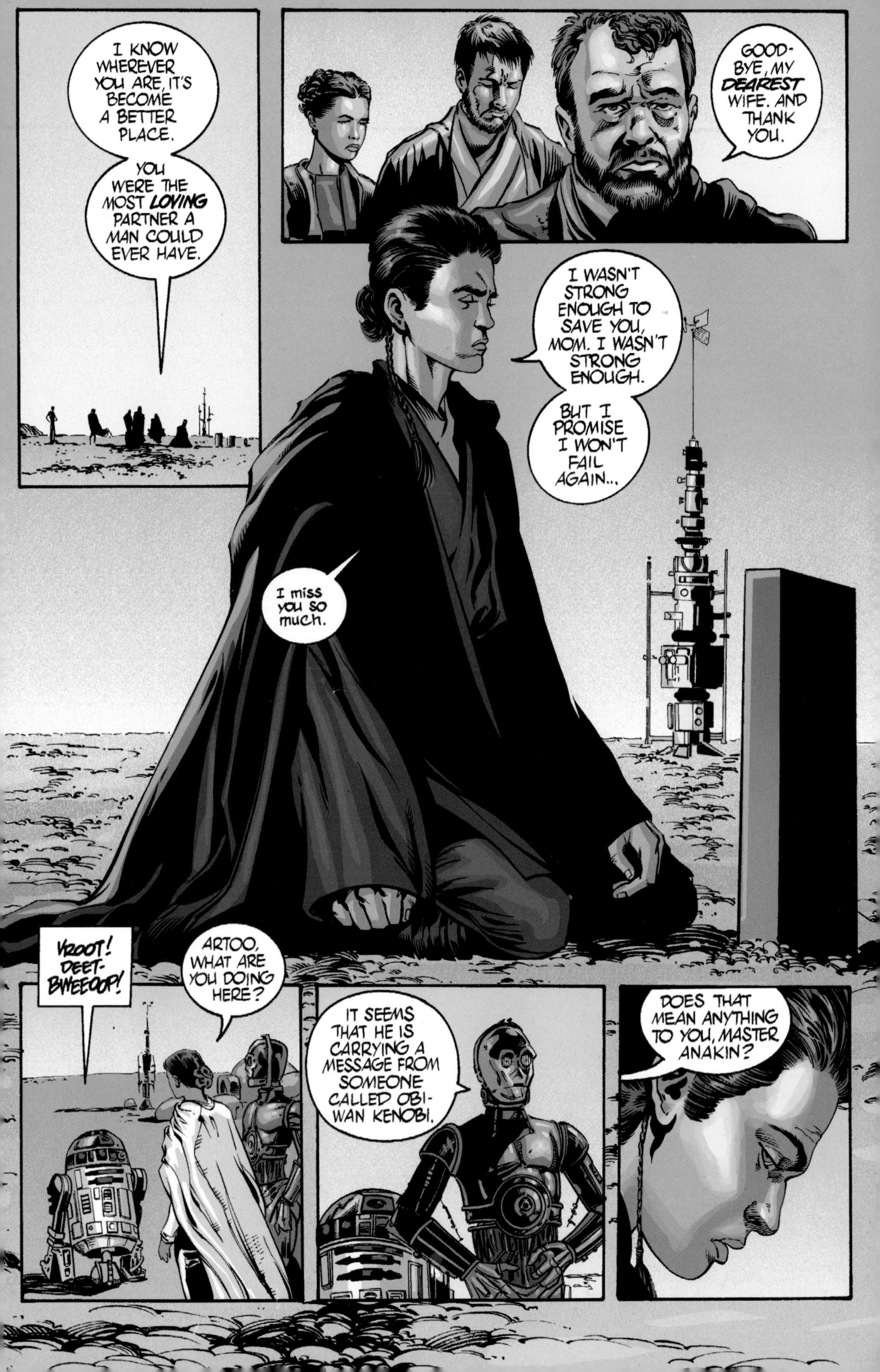
I KNOW WHEREVER YOU ARE, IT'S BECOME A BETTER PLACE.
YOU WERE THE MOST LOVING PARTNER A MAN COULD EVER HAVE.
GOOD-BYE, MY DEAREST WIFE. AND THANK YOU.
I WASN'T STRONG ENOUGH TO SAVE YOU, MOM. I WASN'T STRONG ENOUGH.
BUT I PROMISE I WON'T FAIL AGAIN...
I miss you so much.
VROOT! DEET-BWEEOOP!
ARTOO, WHAT ARE YOU DOING HERE?
IT SEEMS THAT HE IS CARRYING A MESSAGE FROM SOMEONE CALLED OBI-WAN KENOBI.
DOES THAT MEAN ANYTHING TO YOU, MASTER ANAKIN?

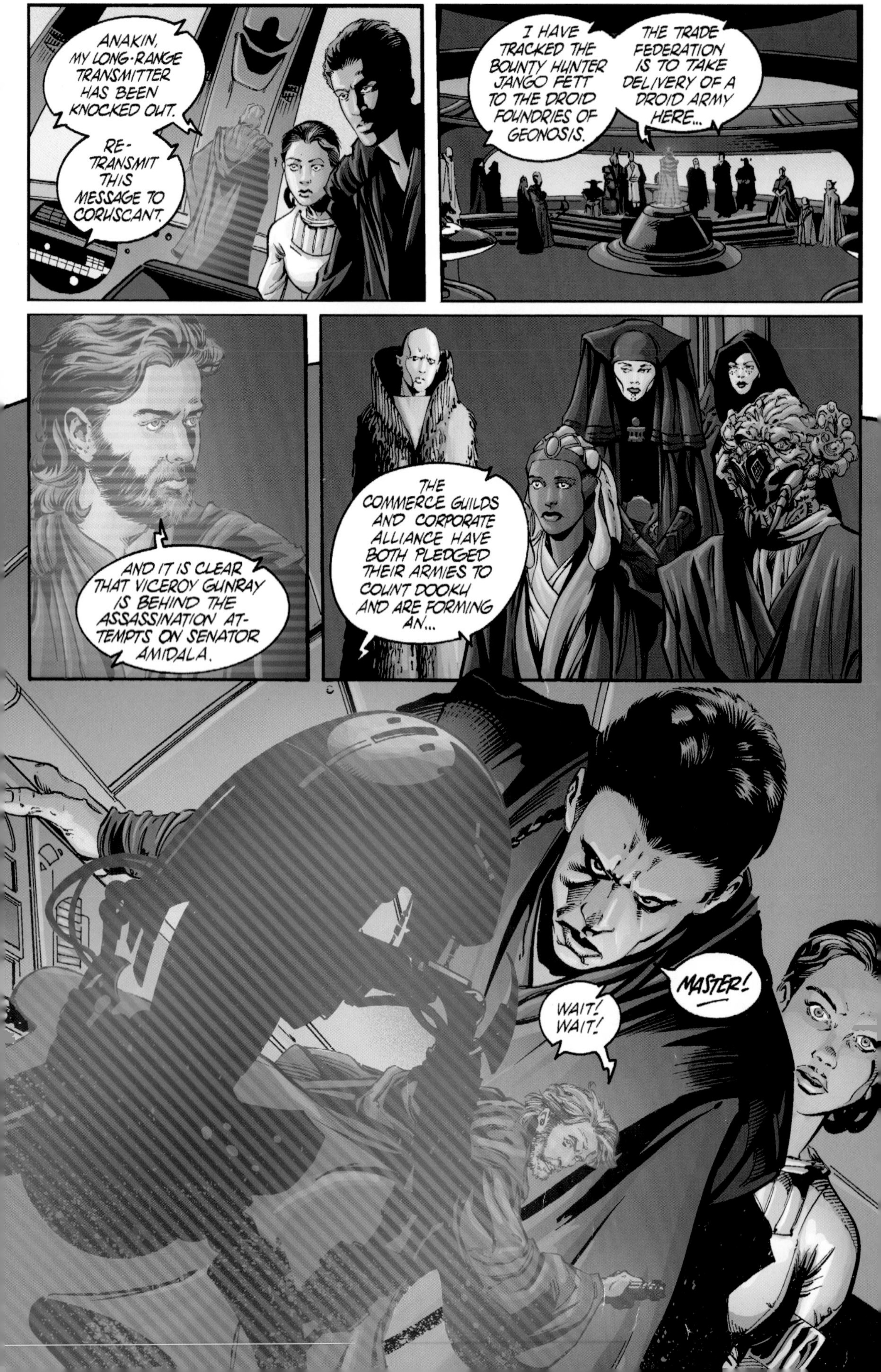
ANAKIN, MY LONG-RANGE TRANSMITTER HAS BEEN KNOCKED OUT.
RE-TRANSMIT THIS MESSAGE TO CORUSCANT.
I HAVE TRACKED THE BOUNTY HUNTER JANGO FETT TO THE DROID FOUNDRIES OF GEONOSIS.
THE TRADE FEDERATION IS TO TAKE DELIVERY OF A DROID ARMY HERE...
AND IT IS CLEAR THAT VICEROY GUNRAY IS BEHIND THE ASSASSINATION AT-TEMPTS ON SENATOR AMIDALA.
THE COMMERCE GUILDS AND CORPORATE ALLIANCE HAVE BOTH PLEDGED THEIR ARMIES TO COUNT DOOKU AND ARE FORMING AN...
MASTER!
WAIT! WAIT!

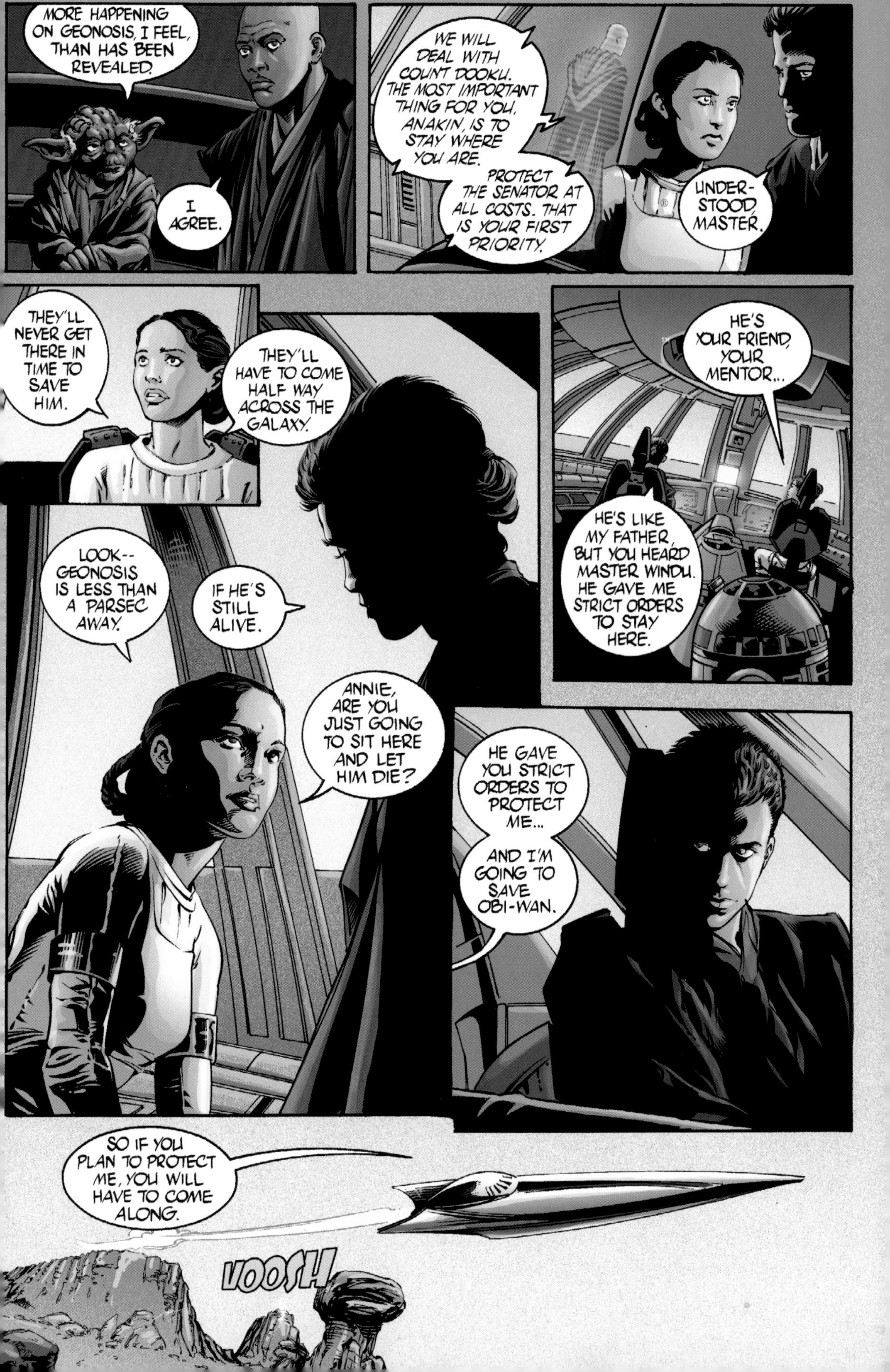
MORE HAPPENING ON GEONOSIS, I FEEL, THAN HAS BEEN REVEALED.
I AGREE.
WE WILL DEAL WITH COUNT DOOKU. THE MOST IMPORTANT THING FOR YOU, ANAKIN, IS TO STAY WHERE YOU ARE.
PROTECT THE SENATOR AT ALL COSTS. THAT IS YOUR FIRST PRIORITY.
UNDER-STOOD, MASTER.
THEY'LL NEVER GET THERE IN TIME TO SAVE HIM.
THEY'LL HAVE TO COME HALF WAY ACROSS THE GALAXY.
HE'S YOUR FRIEND, YOUR MENTOR...
HE'S LIKE MY FATHER, BUT YOU HEARD MASTER WINDU. HE GAVE ME STRICT ORDERS TO STAY HERE.
LOOK-- GEONOSIS IS LESS THAN A PARSEC AWAY.
IF HE'S STILL ALIVE.
ANNIE, ARE YOU JUST GOING TO SIT HERE AND LET HIM DIE?
HE GAVE YOU STRICT ORDERS TO PROTECT ME...
AND I'M GOING TO SAVE OBI-WAN.
SO IF YOU PLAN TO PROTECT ME, YOU WILL HAVE TO COME ALONG.
VOOSH

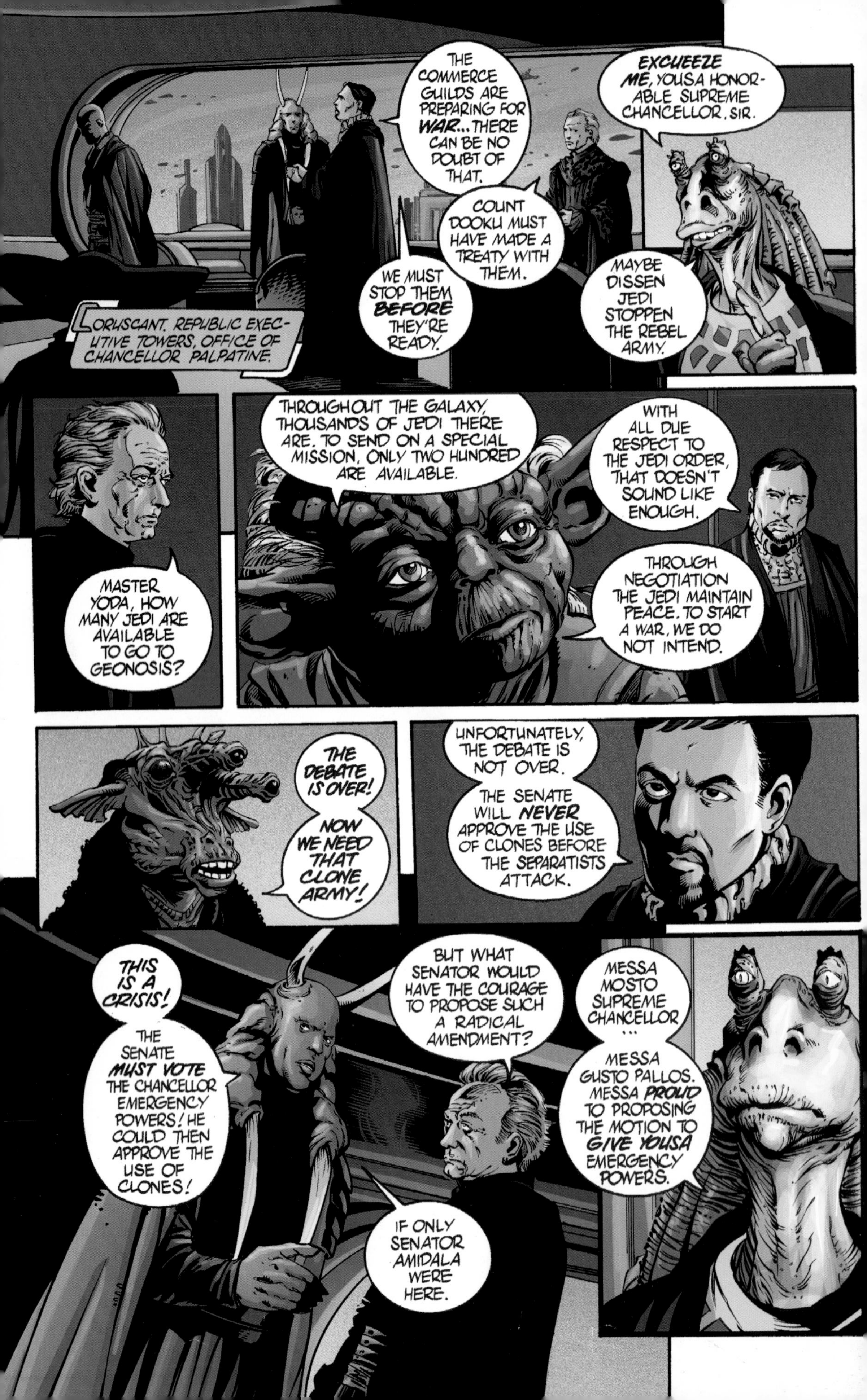

CORUSCANT. REPUBLIC EXECUTIVE TOWERS, OFFICE OF CHANCELLOR PALPATINE.
THE COMMERCE GUILDS ARE PREPARING FOR WAR... THERE CAN BE NO DOUBT OF THAT.
COUNT DOOKU MUST HAVE MADE A TREATY WITH THEM.
WE MUST STOP THEM BEFORE THEY'RE READY.
EXCUEEZE ME, YOUSA HONORABLE SUPREME CHANCELLOR, SIR.
MAYBE DISSEN JEDI STOPPEN THE REBEL ARMY.
MASTER YODA, HOW MANY JEDI ARE AVAILABLE TO GO TO GEONOSIS?
THROUGHOUT THE GALAXY, THOUSANDS OF JEDI THERE ARE. TO SEND ON A SPECIAL MISSION, ONLY TWO HUNDRED ARE AVAILABLE.
WITH ALL DUE RESPECT TO THE JEDI ORDER, THAT DOESN'T SOUND LIKE ENOUGH.
THROUGH NEGOTIATION THE JEDI MAINTAIN PEACE. TO START A WAR, WE DO NOT INTEND.
THE DEBATE IS OVER!
NOW WE NEED THAT CLONE ARMY!
UNFORTUNATELY, THE DEBATE IS NOT OVER.
THE SENATE WILL NEVER APPROVE THE USE OF CLONES BEFORE THE SEPARATISTS ATTACK.
THIS IS A CRISIS!
THE SENATE MUST VOTE THE CHANCELLOR EMERGENCY POWERS! HE COULD THEN APPROVE THE USE OF CLONES!
BUT WHAT SENATOR WOULD HAVE THE COURAGE TO PROPOSE SUCH A RADICAL AMENDMENT?
IF ONLY SENATOR AMIDALA WERE HERE.
MESSA MOSTO SUPREME CHANCELLOR...
MESSA GUSTO PALLOS. MESSA PROUD TO PROPOSING THE MOTION TO GIVE YOUSA EMERGENCY POWERS.

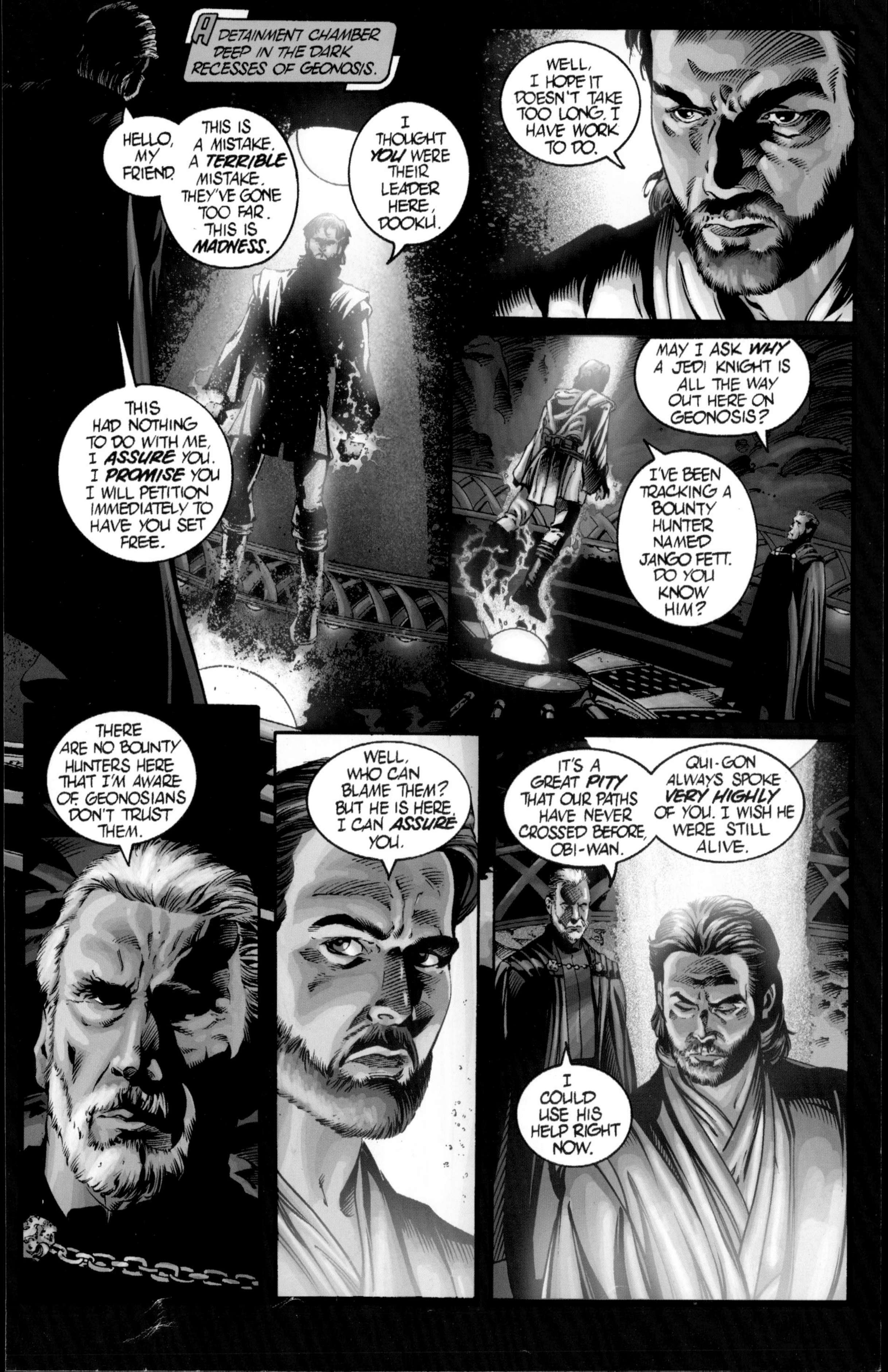
A DETAINMENT CHAMBER DEEP IN THE DARK RECESSES OF GEONOSIS.
HELLO, MY FRIEND.
THIS IS A MISTAKE. A TERRIBLE MISTAKE. THEY'VE GONE TOO FAR. THIS IS MADNESS.
I THOUGHT YOU WERE THEIR LEADER HERE, DOOKU.
WELL, I HOPE IT DOESN'T TAKE TOO LONG. I HAVE WORK TO DO.
THIS HAD NOTHING TO DO WITH ME, I ASSURE YOU. I PROMISE YOU I WILL PETITION IMMEDIATELY TO HAVE YOU SET FREE.
MAY I ASK WHY A JEDI KNIGHT IS ALL THE WAY OUT HERE ON GEONOSIS?
I'VE BEEN TRACKING A BOUNTY HUNTER NAMED JANGO FETT. DO YOU KNOW HIM?
THERE ARE NO BOUNTY HUNTERS HERE THAT I'M AWARE OF. GEONOSIANS DON'T TRUST THEM.
WELL, WHO CAN BLAME THEM? BUT HE IS HERE, I CAN ASSURE YOU.
IT'S A GREAT PITY THAT OUR PATHS HAVE NEVER CROSSED BEFORE, OBI-WAN.
QUI-GON ALWAYS SPOKE VERY HIGHLY OF YOU. I WISH HE WERE STILL ALIVE.
I COULD USE HIS HELP RIGHT NOW.

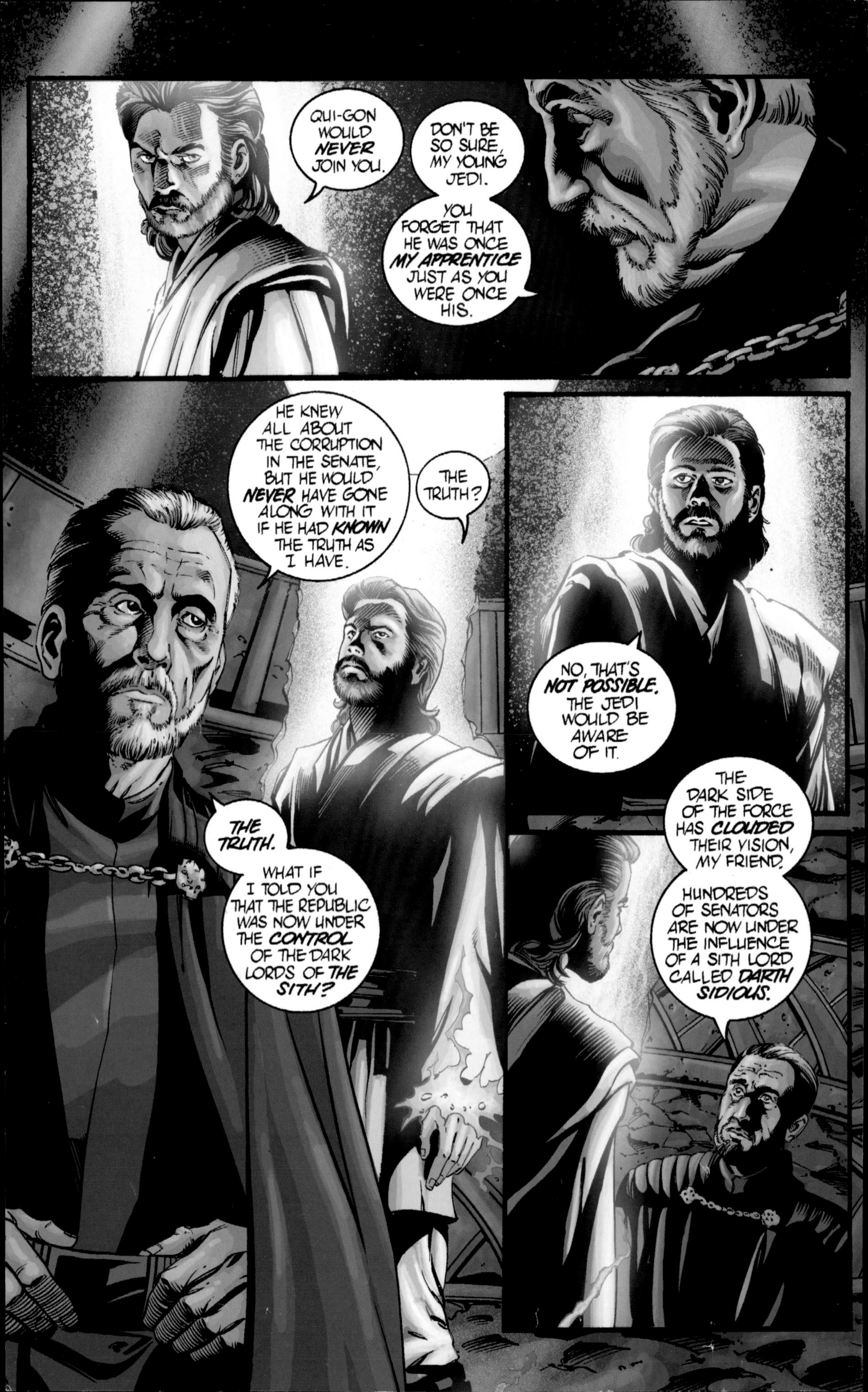
QUI-GON WOULD **NEVER** JOIN YOU.
DON'T BE SO SURE, MY YOUNG JEDI.
YOU FORGET THAT HE WAS ONCE **MY APPRENTICE** JUST AS YOU WERE ONCE HIS.
HE KNEW ALL ABOUT THE CORRUPTION IN THE SENATE, BUT HE WOULD **NEVER** HAVE GONE ALONG WITH IT IF HE HAD **KNOWN** THE TRUTH AS I HAVE.
THE TRUTH?
THE TRUTH.
WHAT IF I TOLD YOU THAT THE REPUBLIC WAS NOW UNDER THE **CONTROL** OF THE DARK LORDS OF **THE SITH?**
NO, THAT'S **NOT POSSIBLE.** THE JEDI WOULD BE AWARE OF IT.
THE DARK SIDE OF THE FORCE HAS **CLOUDED** THEIR VISION, MY FRIEND.
HUNDREDS OF SENATORS ARE NOW UNDER THE INFLUENCE OF A SITH LORD CALLED **DARTH SIDIOUS.**

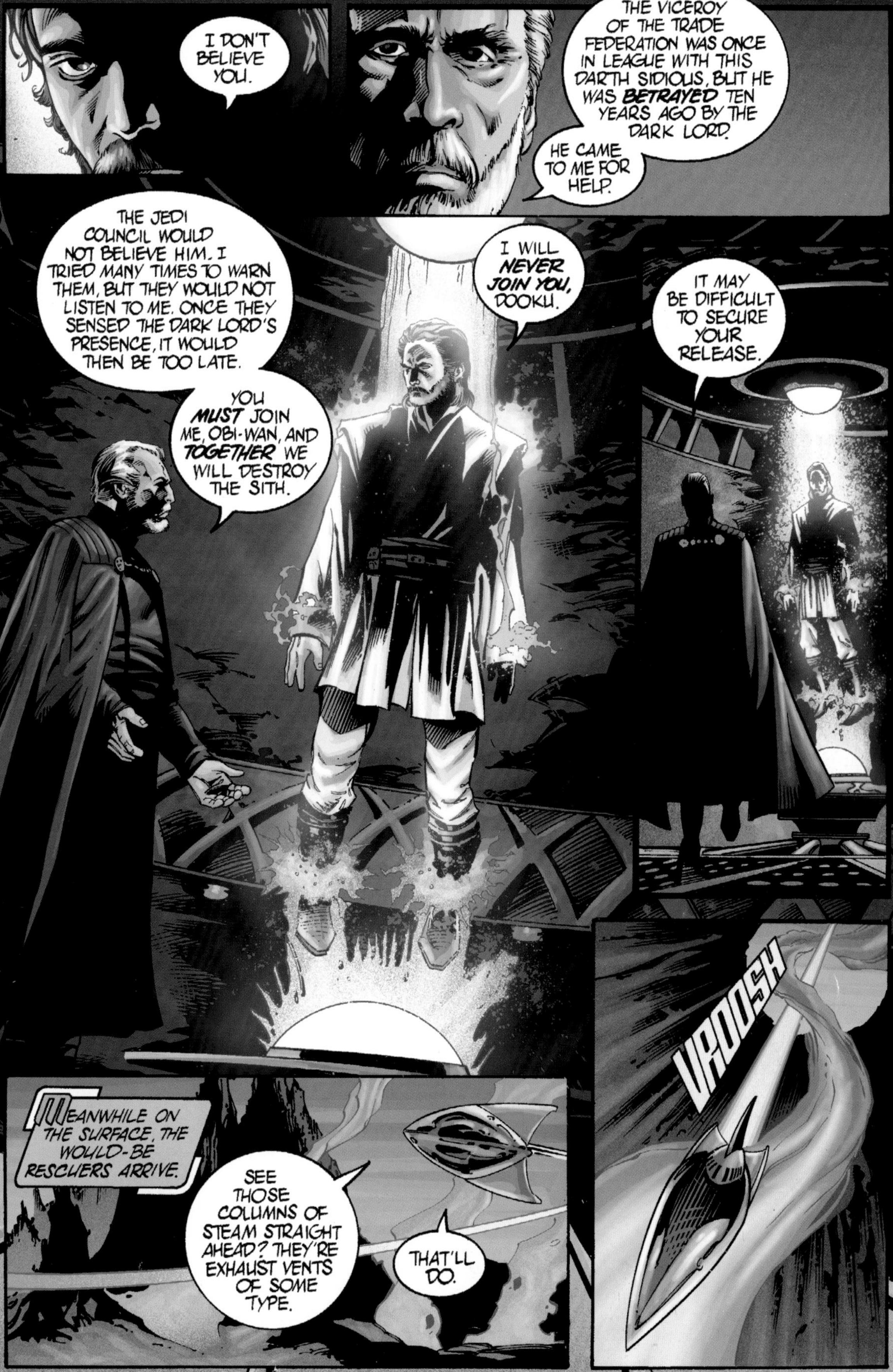
I DON'T BELIEVE YOU.
THE VICEROY OF THE TRADE FEDERATION WAS ONCE IN LEAGUE WITH THIS DARTH SIDIOUS, BUT HE WAS BETRAYED TEN YEARS AGO BY THE DARK LORD.
HE CAME TO ME FOR HELP.
THE JEDI COUNCIL WOULD NOT BELIEVE HIM. I TRIED MANY TIMES TO WARN THEM, BUT THEY WOULD NOT LISTEN TO ME. ONCE THEY SENSED THE DARK LORD'S PRESENCE, IT WOULD THEN BE TOO LATE.
YOU MUST JOIN ME, OBI-WAN, AND TOGETHER WE WILL DESTROY THE SITH.
I WILL NEVER JOIN YOU, DOOKU.
IT MAY BE DIFFICULT TO SECURE YOUR RELEASE.
MEANWHILE ON THE SURFACE, THE WOULD-BE RESCUERS ARRIVE.
SEE THOSE COLUMNS OF STEAM STRAIGHT AHEAD? THEY'RE EXHAUST VENTS OF SOME TYPE.
THAT'LL DO.
VROOSH

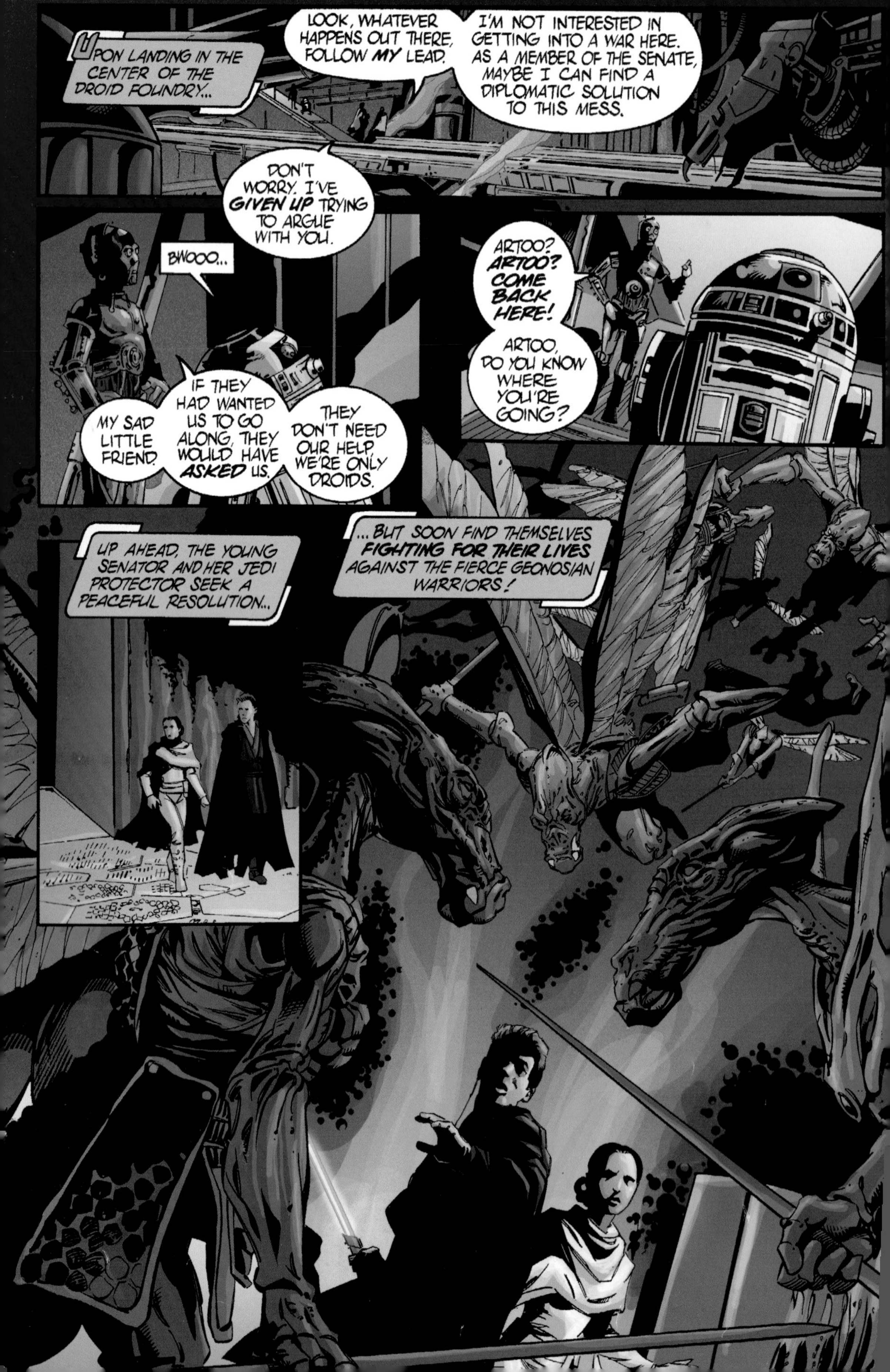
UPON LANDING IN THE CENTER OF THE DROID FOUNDRY...
LOOK, WHATEVER HAPPENS OUT THERE, FOLLOW MY LEAD.
I'M NOT INTERESTED IN GETTING INTO A WAR HERE. AS A MEMBER OF THE SENATE, MAYBE I CAN FIND A DIPLOMATIC SOLUTION TO THIS MESS.
DON'T WORRY. I'VE GIVEN UP TRYING TO ARGUE WITH YOU.
BWOOO...
MY SAD LITTLE FRIEND.
IF THEY HAD WANTED US TO GO ALONG, THEY WOULD HAVE ASKED US.
THEY DON'T NEED OUR HELP. WE'RE ONLY DROIDS.
ARTOO? ARTOO? COME BACK HERE!
ARTOO, DO YOU KNOW WHERE YOU'RE GOING?
UP AHEAD, THE YOUNG SENATOR AND HER JEDI PROTECTOR SEEK A PEACEFUL RESOLUTION...
...BUT SOON FIND THEMSELVES FIGHTING FOR THEIR LIVES AGAINST THE FIERCE GEONOSIAN WARRIORS!

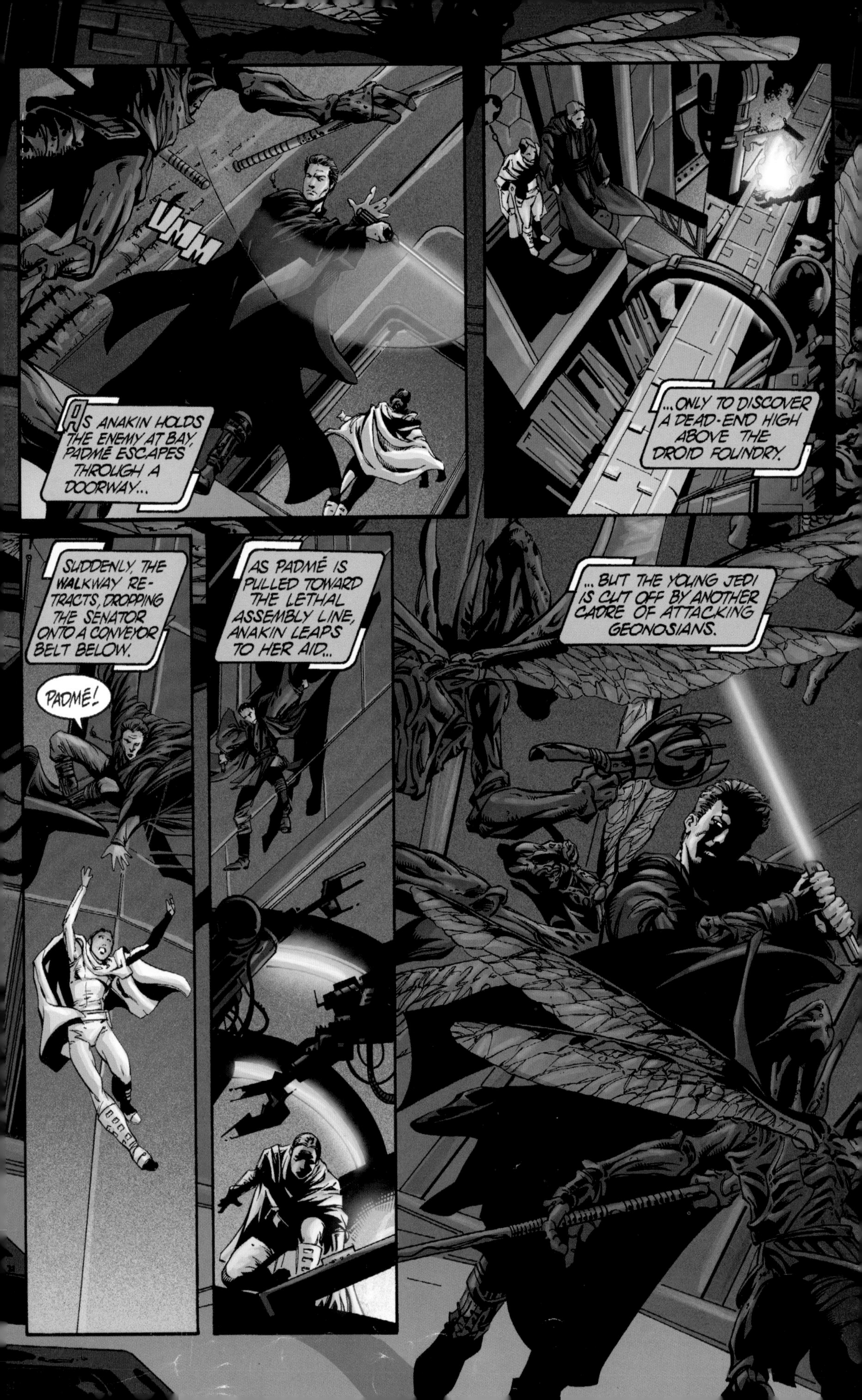
UMM
AS ANAKIN HOLDS THE ENEMY AT BAY, PADMÉ ESCAPES THROUGH A DOORWAY...
...ONLY TO DISCOVER A DEAD-END HIGH ABOVE THE DROID FOUNDRY.
SUDDENLY, THE WALKWAY RE-TRACTS, DROPPING THE SENATOR ONTO A CONVEYOR BELT BELOW.
PADMÉ!
AS PADMÉ IS PULLED TOWARD THE LETHAL ASSEMBLY LINE, ANAKIN LEAPS TO HER AID...
...BUT THE YOUNG JEDI IS CUT OFF BY ANOTHER CADRE OF ATTACKING GEONOSIANS.

LAGGING BEHIND, R2-D2 AND C-3PO FINALLY REACH THE ELEVATED WALKWAY...

ARTOO! THERE'S NOWHERE LEFT TO GO!

BWEEP!

JUMP? I AM NOT GOING TO JUMP!

OHH!

PANG

FOOSH

OH! THIS IS ALL YOUR FAULT!

MEANWHILE, IN THE MIDST OF THE SMELTING VATS, A GEONOSIAN AMBUSHES PADMÉ, WITH DISASTROUS RESULTS!

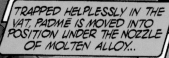

EEEE!

FOOSH

TRAPPED HELPLESSLY IN THE VAT, PADMÉ IS MOVED INTO POSITION UNDER THE NOZZLE OF MOLTEN ALLOY...

AS IT PREPARES TO UNLEASH ITS SCORCHING PAYLOAD.

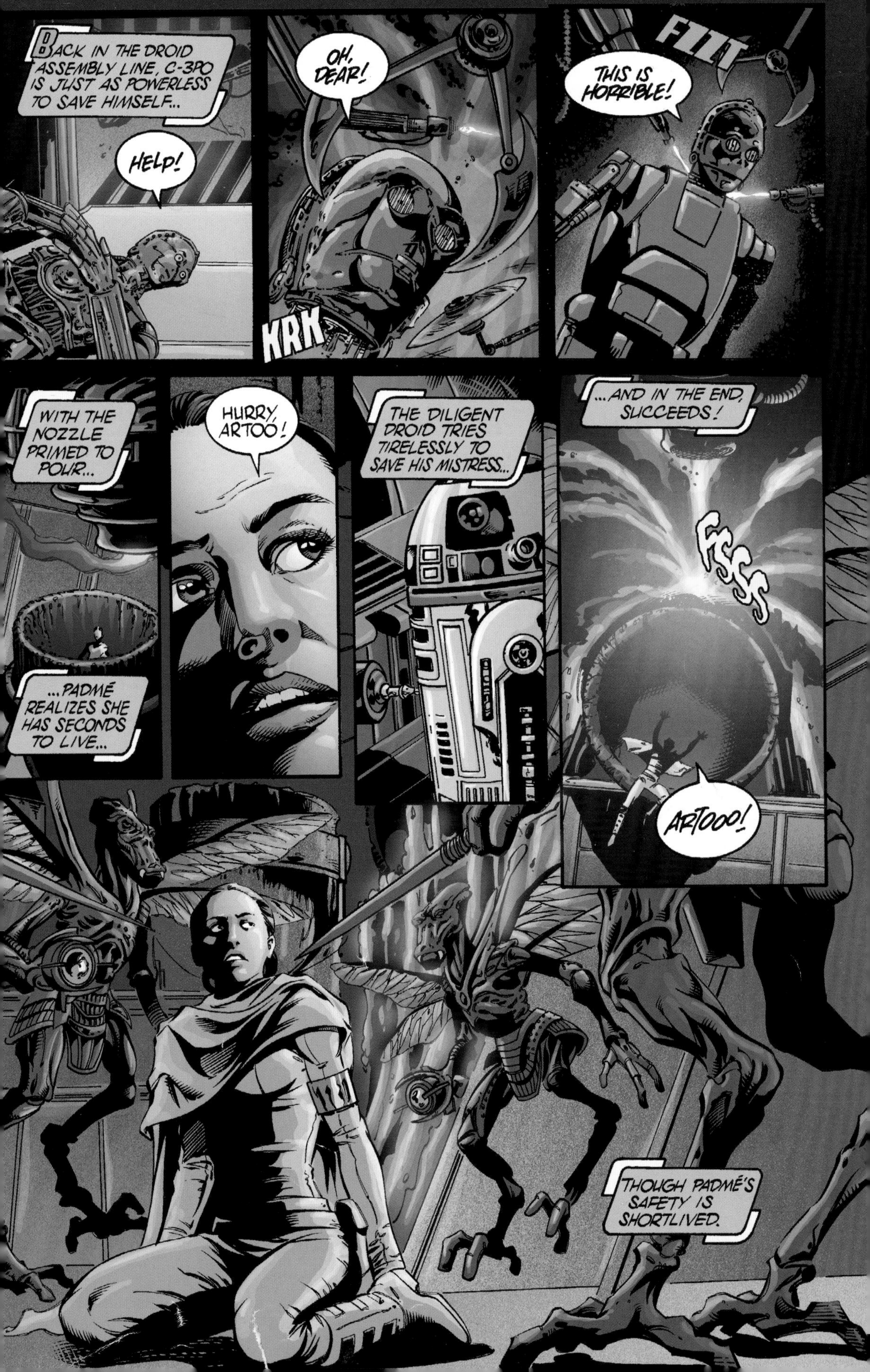
BACK IN THE DROID ASSEMBLY LINE, C-3PO IS JUST AS POWERLESS TO SAVE HIMSELF...
HELP!
OH, DEAR!
KRK
FZZT
THIS IS HORRIBLE!
WITH THE NOZZLE PRIMED TO POUR...
...PADMÉ REALIZES SHE HAS SECONDS TO LIVE...
HURRY, ARTOO!
THE DILIGENT DROID TRIES TIRELESSLY TO SAVE HIS MISTRESS...
...AND IN THE END, SUCCEEDS!
FSSS
ARTOOO!
THOUGH PADMÉ'S SAFETY IS SHORTLIVED.

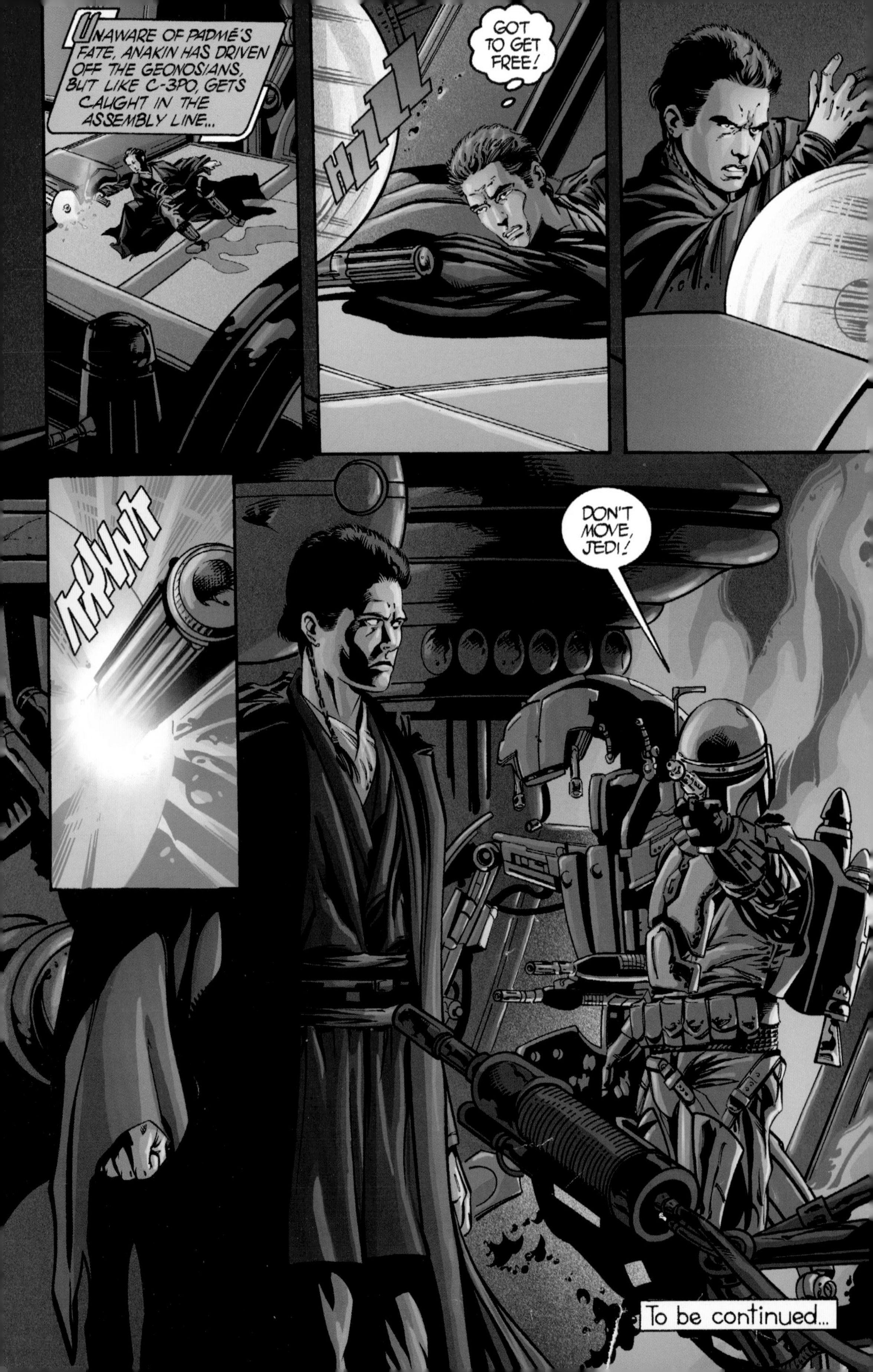
UNAWARE OF PADMÉ'S FATE, ANAKIN HAS DRIVEN OFF THE GEONOSIANS, BUT LIKE C-3PO, GETS CAUGHT IN THE ASSEMBLY LINE...
HZZZ
GOT TO GET FREE!
KRUNT
DON'T MOVE, JEDI!
To be continued...

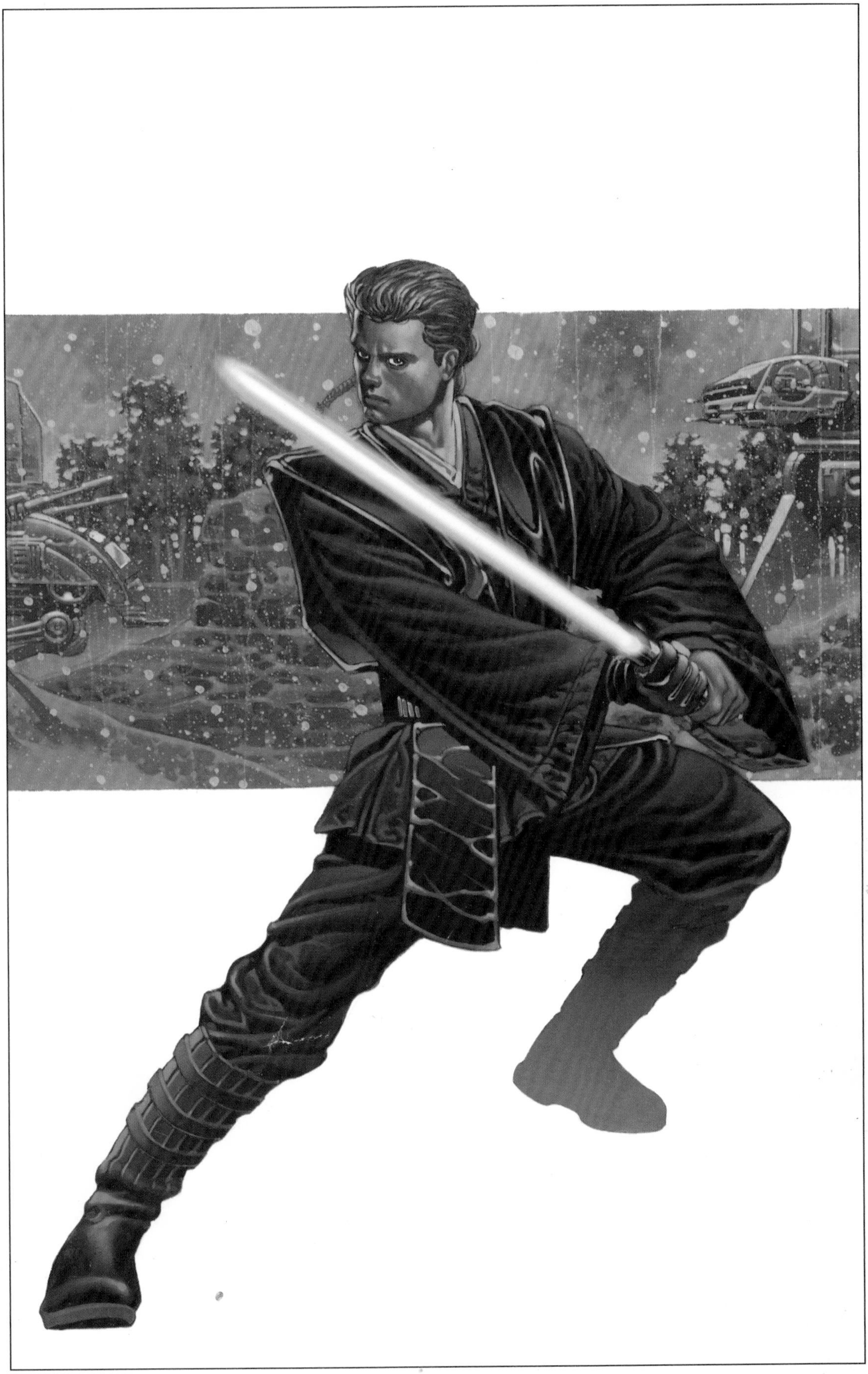

ART BY CARLO ARRELLANO

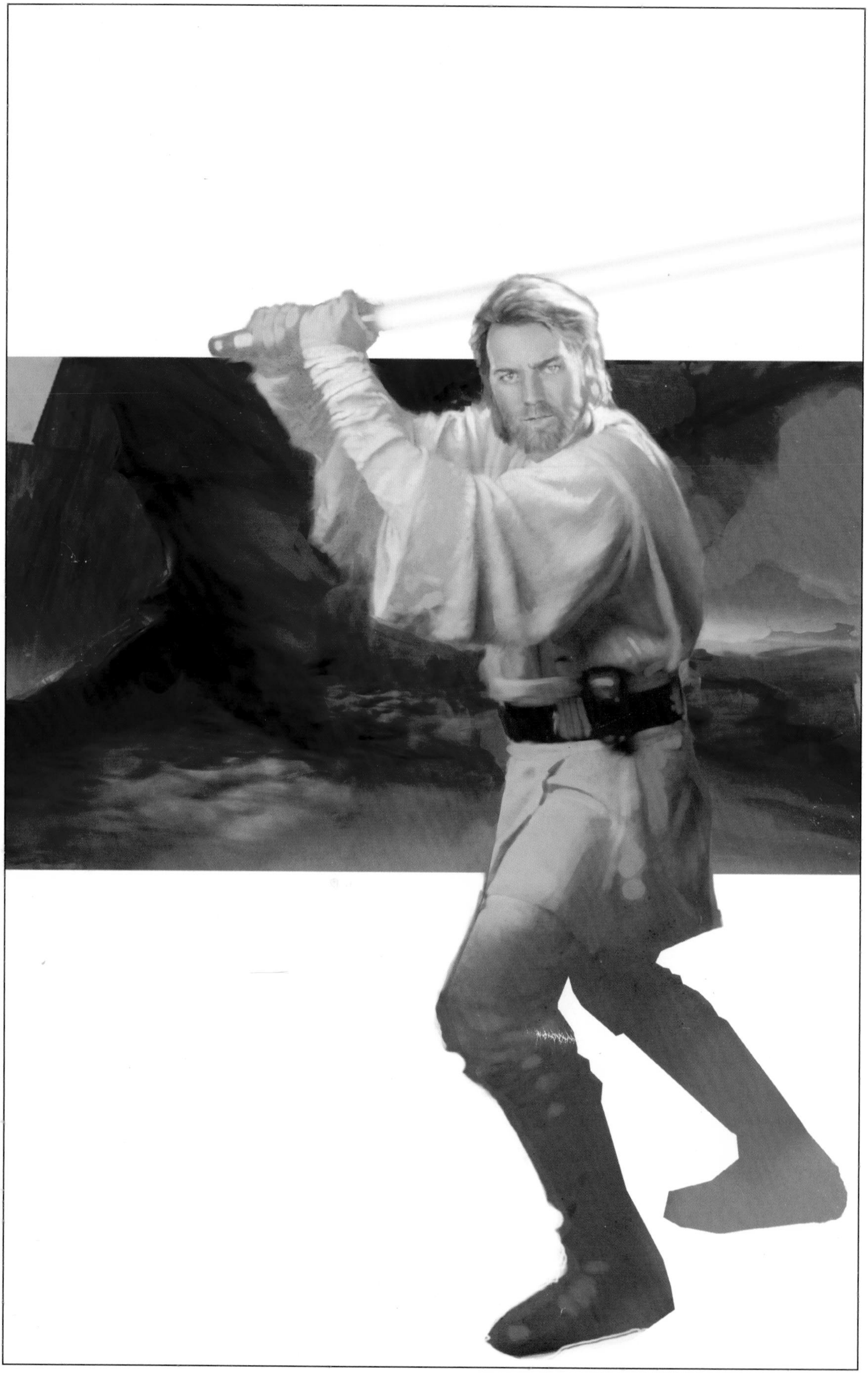

ART BY **CARLO ARRELLANO**